The
Turning
Point

The Turning Point

Best of Young Indian Writers

edited by
Nikita Singh

Offshoots

© Individual contributors, 2014
Concept: Shobit Arya

First published 2014
Reprinted 2015

ISBN 978-81-8328-356-4

Published by
Wisdom Tree
4779/23, Ansari Road
Darya Ganj, New Delhi-110 002
Ph.: 23247966/67/68
wisdomtreebooks@gmail.com

Printed in India

CONTENTS

EDITOR'S NOTE

When this book was conceived, the idea was to get some of the best young Indian writers together, and have them write short stories, without binding them to a central theme. Letting everyone do their own thing—that's the crux of it. One thing I noticed was how all these writers have moved beyond their established genre and explored new frontiers, pushing the boundaries.

That is what I believe is responsible for the exciting mix of genre and style in this book. Every story follows its own way, without a predefined pattern. As you go from one story to another, you get transported from one world to an entirely different one.

Meenakshi Reddy Madhavan's *Insert a Carrot* is full of humour and wit, and provides a brilliant insight into modern day relationships, break ups and all things related. Durjoy Datta's *The English Teacher* explores the age old fascination of school students with their teachers...taking it to another level altogether. Judy Balan's *The Return of the (Original) Vampire* is a quirky take on the present day picturisation of vampires. Harsh Snehanshu writes about first love and destiny in *Summer Showers*. Shoma Narayanan has written a hilarious story about a ghost, that hangs back in the real world, in *The X-Boss*. Parinda joshi's *An Unlikely Accomplice* is a crime thriller, circling around a rave party in the suburbs of Ahmedabad. Atulya Mahajan writes about confusion, uncertainty and realisation in *The U-Turn*. And I have written about moving forward and hope, in *A Whispered Prayer*.

We have a vampire going through identity crisis, a ghost stuck in the real world, a closet psychopath and a young boy in love. We have a girl moving on after a break up, an uncle coming to terms with his grief and the truth, a to-be father struggling with establishing priorities and a rape survivor, dealing with ghosts from her past.

The one thing all stories have in common is a turning point. Every story starts or ends at a turning point. Or maybe revolves around one. Things change—that's one truth of life. As John Green writes in *The Fault in Our Stars*, 'Grief does not change you. It reveals you.' Life is about accepting things that don't happen our way and take them in our stride. It is only when we go through certain things in life that we discover what really matters to us and what should not. I think this is what most stories here talk about.

I have had a great time working with all these amazing writers, and I do hope you like reading the stories as much as I enjoyed working on them. Please feel free to connect with the writers, and me at any time for suggestions, comments and—the best of all—appreciation!

INSERT A CARROT

MEENAKSHI REDDY MADHAVAN

- I don't think it says what it's supposed to say.
- What do you mean? What does it say?
- Oh dear. Oh, you're not going to like this.
- You're seriously freaking me out now, just tell me!
- Okay. OKAY. Just remember not to shoot the messenger.
- I'll shoot *you* if you don't bloody tell me what's going on.
- There's no 'a'.
- What do you mean there's no 'a'?
- In 'behaved'. There's no 'a'.
- How can there not be an 'a'? I saw the stencil! The stencil totally had an 'a'.
- Well, this doesn't.
- Are you sure? Do you have a mirror?

- How long have you known me? Do I look like the kind of person to carry a mirror?

- Oh my God. Are you really making this about you at this point? Just find something! A reflective surface! I have to see it!

- There *are* no reflective surfaces! Oh—wait, I have an idea, let me take a picture with my phone and show it to you.

- Done?

- Hang on, wait, yeah, there it is. It's a bit blurry, but...

- OH MY GOD.

- I'm sorry!

- OH MY FREAKING GOD!

- I'm sure it can be fixed!

- Why were you not looking when he did it?

- I was holding your hand, remember? You said to distract you!

- Yes, but you could've checked when he was done.

- This is *not* my fault.

- Oh. My. God.

- Relax.

- Don't tell me to relax. I'm having a panic attack. I can't breathe.

- If you couldn't breathe, you wouldn't be talking.

- Is this the time? No, really, *is it?*

- You could put that thing, what's it called? The upward arrow thing?
- A carrot?
- Is it really called a carrot?
- Something like that.
- Well, anyway, you could put the carrot and put the 'a' in, and I think it would look quite good.
- It would look sloppy.
- Well, either that, or you could have it laser removed and re-do it.
- How much would a laser removal cost?
- More than *that* did, that's for sure.
- Oh great. Now I'm stuck with it.
- You know, you can only tell it's misspelled if you look *really* closely.
- It's on my lower back.
- So?
- Sooo, that means I kinda *want* people—the right people—to look at it closely.
- They call it a tramp stamp.
- Who calls it a tramp stamp?
- People. About people with tattoos on their lower backs.
- You couldn't have told me this before?
- I assumed you knew. This is common pop culture knowledge.

- I don't watch as much TV as you do!
- Hey, my TV has just pointed out that you have a tramp stamp.
- A *misspelled* tramp stamp.
- Don't cry.
- Who's crying?
- You looked like you were about to.
- I'm not crying; I'm angry at the stupid tattoo artist.
- Maybe if you had spent less time flirting with him, he could have concentrated on his job.
- I was *so* not flirting with him!
- Yuh-huh. You so were!
- I was being polite. Here's a life lesson: when someone is holding a needle to your skin, you should normally try to be polite.
- Otherwise they might mess things up?
- Yes—oh, shut up.
- We'll go back. We'll put in the carrot.
- Is there space for the carrot?
- Yes, I think so. Listen, are you sure it's called a carrot?
- Let me Google it.
- What? What?
- Oh God.
- *What?*

- Another life lesson: never search on Google for 'insert carrot'.

- …

- Don't laugh! This is not funny!

- It's *hysterical*!

- I'm glad my fate brings you so much amusement.

- Oh, don't be a drama queen. Let me search.

- What are you searching for?

- Definitely not 'insert carrot', that's for sure. No, I'm searching for 'symbol to insert a missing letter.'

- Oh.

- Yeah.

- I would have thought of that, it's just, you know, the stress.

- Of course, darling. Don't beat yourself up.

- Did you find it?

- Yes! And here's good news, you were right! Doesn't that cheer you up?

- It's called a carrot?

- Close. It's called a car*et*.

- Carrot. Like I said.

- No, no. Caret. Like diamonds.

- But diamonds have carrots too.

- Wow.

- What?
- I can't believe you just said that.
- *What?*
- You honestly don't know the difference between a carrot—vegetable and a car*et*—diamond?
- It sounds like you're saying exactly the same thing.
- CarET, you deaf idiot! Et! Et!
- Would you keep your voice down?
- I cannot possibly fathom how you have spent your whole life saying 'carrot' and no one has corrected you.
- It sounds the same to me.
- Repeat after me: C
- This is ridiculous.
- Repeat, I said!
- 'C'
- Very good! 'A'.
- 'A'
- 'R'
- Is this necessary?
- R!
- Arrrrrrr.
- 'E'
- 'E'
- 'T'!

- T
- And that's how you spell 'caret'.
- That's just great, Nush, thanks.
- What?
- We're meant to be focusing on my misery here, not giving me a spelling lesson.
- But the spelling lesson will be so important when you go back to the tattoo artist.
- Why?
- Because, imagine if you told him to insert a carrot and he already thought you were flirting with him and—ow!
- You deserved that.
- It's fun-*neee*.
- It's *on my body*.
- But imagine the fun times you'll have when a boy undresses you and he says, 'What's that?' and you'll say, 'Well, I inserted a carrot.'
- Well.
- Hah! You totally want to smile! I see it.
- I'm probably smiling out of despair.
- No, I know your despairing smile, this is your I'm-trying-not-to-laugh-and-failing-smile.
- You know, this *would* happen. The Universe hates me. I am no longer a Beloved Child of the Universe. I'm like the Universe's Stepdaughter.

- Stepdaughters get away with a lot. And they get to marry the prince.

- Hah.

- I said, 'get to', I didn't say they *did*.

- Be that as it may. What is the protocol on break ups?

- We've discussed this, and there are no hard and fast rules…

- Still! What is the one, standard, universal break up protocol?

- That one or both members of the breakup do something drastic to their appearance.

- And what has Abhi done?

- Do we really want to talk about Abhi?

- Just answer the question.

- He got a haircut.

- A haircut! He had dreadlocks! His dreadlocks were his *thing*. I might have even dated him *for* his dreadlocks!

- Really?

- Don't be judgy, Miss I-Went-Out-With-a-Walking-Heart-Attack.

- He was *not*.

- He was three times your size!

- You are such a size-ist!

- How did you even have sex with him is what I want to know.

- You *know*.
- I just want you to say it again.
- Fine. On top.
- A-ha!
- I *like* being on top.
- Correction: you *had* to be on top. Or he would've squished you. Like a bug.
- Well, at least he didn't look like a caveman.
- Abhi was very sexy.
- If you like Neolithic men.
- Homo *erectus*, if you know what I mean.
- Oh God, you're disgusting.
- I'm also never going to have sex again.
- Oh, sweetie, don't say that, you'll be back on the horse in no time.
- No, I mean it. I'm never taking my clothes off again.
- The right man will not notice your carrot.
- Please don't say it, I beg you.
- In fact, he might come with his *own* carrot.
- You said it.
- It was right there, waiting to be said. It would've been like the elephant in the bedroom.
- Huh.
- Or the donkey, in this case, because I don't think elephants eat carrots.

- D'you think Abhi's having a lot of sex?

- Maya…

- No, I mean, think about it. There were probably loads of girls, like you, before, who'd have been all like, 'Oh, he'd be cute if he lost the dreadlocks.' And now that he *has*, there must be all these girls just like *throwing* themselves at him.

- He wasn't all that, with or without dreadlocks.

- People used to look at us, you know? They'd look at us when we walked into a party or a bar or something, the girls would all look at him and then look at me, and I could see them wondering, 'What's someone like that doing with *her*?'

- Or, very probably, they thought, 'What's someone like *her* doing with *that*?'

- You're sweet.

- I'm honest! Listen; I know what you're going through, I broke up with Mayank not too long ago.

- Fat Mayank.

- Yes, okay, Fat Mayank, but I really liked him.

- I know you did.

- You have some weird fat issues, but I happen to like my men cuddly.

- Nothing wrong with that! Fly that fat flag high, sister!

- *Any*way. Even though things with me and Mayank…

- Fat Mayank.

- Really? Okay, you're blue, I'll give you this much. Even though things with me and *Fat* Mayank were never stellar, I kinda hoped that one day they would be. So it hurt when things ended.
- And you joined a gym.
- And I joined a gym, and it was a very good decision.
- You look fabulous, did I tell you that already? You look absolutely stunning today.
- Thank you, my love, and so do you.
- With a misspelled tattoo on my ass.
- Technically, it's your lower back, and hey, even if it *is* misspelled, it looks nice.
- Really?
- Oh totally. The font looks great!
- I suppose that's small compensation.
- It's great compensation. You wouldn't like a tacky font on your back, would you?
- I did spend a lot of time choosing the script.
- *We* spent a lot of time choosing the script.
- Oh, Nush.
- What is it?
- Nothing. You've been great. *So* great.
- You're not going to get all sentimental on me, are you?
- Is there something wrong with someone thanking their friend?

- Friendship means never having to say thank you. Or something.

- Isn't that a line from *Love Story*?

- Yes, yes it is. It's 'Love means never having to say you're sorry.'

- God, I hated that book.

- Did you? I loved it when I was a teenager. I worshipped it. I swooned over it. I thought I was the first person ever to have cried when poor Jenny died.

- I thought I did too, but then I re-read it, and I was like, 'Man, this book is stupid.' I mean, *Love means never having to say you're sorry*? That sounds like a recipe for disaster to me. If you ask me, people should apologise more often.

- Are we thinking of certain people?

- Aren't we always? God, I've become such a girl with a one track mind. All I can think about is Abhi, Abhi, Abhi. I don't know what's wrong with me.

- It's natural. I mean, you *did* just break up with him.

- Yeah, but before him, I was perfectly fine. I was smart! I had thoughts beyond, 'Who is my ex-boyfriend doing today?'

- You'll get over it.

- I don't think you get it, it's like, the stuff I tell you is only half the stuff! I wake up in the morning and I check his Facebook profile. If he has new friends, I click through to see if any of them are pretty young single girls. I listen to the playlist he made me, and I cry. There is something wrong with me.

- You know when Fat Mayank—there, see, I said it, are you happy?—when Fat Mayank and I broke up, I spent the week in one of the T-shirts he left behind, because it still smelt of him, and I walked around the house in this T-shirt.

- Which must have been like a dress on you!

- It was rather big, yeah, and I'd hold it to my face and I'd sniff, because he used this really nice cologne and the T-shirt still smelt a little bit of him, and this would be like, what? Three in the morning? And then by four, I'd be hungry, so I'd make Maggi noodles or something, and I'd sit there, in this T-shirt, eating Maggi noodles and feeling like a pathetic loser.

- Then what happened?

- Then? My maid found it and washed it, and the smell was gone.

- You never told me you did that.

- Yes, well, you were in your Abhi bubble, and no one likes to hear their friend's sad stories when they're in their happy place.

- I would've listened.

- I know you would have. I just, I just felt like holding on to the sorrow for myself for a while.

- I get that.
- Do you?
- Yeah, because, the pain, it's not great, but it's still *ours*, you know? It belongs to us, me and Abhi, and it's the last bit I'll ever have of us together.
- Wow, we're morbid.
- I know.
- Morbid bitches.
- I *know*!
- You do realise, right, that neither Fat Mayank nor Abhi are sitting around sniffing our T-shirts or playing our music?
- They're still stalking us on Facebook though.
- Oh totally.
- What did we do before Facebook?
- We depended on the not-so-authentic news reports of our friends.
- Oh my God, remember Jasleen?
- That girl had issues.
- Remember how when we broke up with—what were their names?
- Farad and Hiten.
- *Farad and Hiten.* Yes. And then she came up to us the next day and she told us she had seen both of them at her local park hooking up with two new girls?

- And we bought it.
- Even though her local park was like *miles* away from where they actually lived.
- Why were we dating them?
- Because they were best friends, and we were best friends, and it just made everything so convenient.
- Ah yes, convenience. That all-important factor for romance.
- It just made things easier though. One car. One date. Our parents were cool knowing we were out with each other.
- Did you and Hiten ever…?
- Once. When we went to watch *The Matrix*. He put his hand on my boob.
- Wow. You *slut*.
- Quite. Did you and Farad?
- He kissed really badly. Like, his tongue was everywhere at once.
- Ew.
- I know. It was like making out with an octopus.
- Ewwww.
- Well, you *asked*.
- At least his bad kissing made it easy for you to break up with him, making it that much easier for me to end things with ol' Hiten.

- Are you kidding? Bad kisser or not, *he* dumped *me*.
- *No!*
- He totally did. One day, I think we all had just gone for dinner, and before we got into the car, Farad took me aside and said, 'Anushka, ya, I'm really sorry, ya, but like, I don't want to be your boyfriend anymore.'
- What an asshole!
- I was a bit relieved, to tell the truth. But my dainty little ego was all crushed, so I took that to mean I really liked him.
- What did you *do*?
- Well, I asked him why, and he said there was someone else.
- Someone *else*? Who else would date him?
- His neighbour, apparently. She'd been giving him the come-on for a while, and once he was sure he'd never make it below my neck, he decided to cut his losses.
- Well, Hiten and I never knew.
- Hiten liked you.
- I liked him too, but you know, half the fun was us all dating together.
- You make us sound like a commune.
- It was a little bit, except really sexless.
- Imagine a foursome with those two.
- Oh God.

- I'm sorry!
- Oh. God.
- I'm really sorry, I don't know what made me say it.
- Now I have mental *images.*
- If it makes you feel any better, so do I.
- I wonder what their penises would look like.
- Maya!
- What? Don't tell me you never thought about it.
- May I remind you, while you were getting all that boob groping action, I was still a good girl, sitting with my legs crossed.
- Still, I mean, think about it. When you think of a guy, if you know what he's like as a person, it's pretty easy to imagine his penis.
- You think?
- Oh sure. I'm pretty sure I can come up with an accurate image of the member of every single man we know.
- All right. Let's try it. What do you think Hiten's would look like?
- Sort of…skinny?
- Pencil-like?
- Oh God, those are the worst! It's like fiddling about in you.
- Like a cocktail stirrer? Men don't get that it's not all about the length, it's mostly the girth.

- Sometimes length is important too, I mean, I bet Farad's would be like, the opposite. He'd have a teeny weenie.

- Like a cocktail sausage.

- Do you want a drink or something? Only, that's the second time you've used the cocktail imagery vis-a-vis the penis.

- I'd love a drink. But I'm liking this game.

- There's only one way to tell if I'm right though.

- What's that?

- You're not going to like it.

- Oh, go on.

- I'm going to have to imagine Fat Mayank's penis.

- Like you haven't before.

- I restrained myself. *Massive* restraint.

- Okay.

- Really? No take-backs?

- Nope. Hit me. What do you think Fat Mayank's penis would look like?

- Fat. And squirmy. And pale. Like a maggot.

- Wrong!

- Really?

- You really *are* a size-ist. Why do you think I was with him for so long?

- *Rea-lleeee?*

- Oh yeah. Beautiful craftsmanship.
- No kidding. Huh. Go, Fat Mayank!
- What was Abhi's like, then?
- Nush!
- Come on, you got to guess mine.
- I *refuse* to discuss Abhi's penis.
- Big? Small? Short? Fat?
- Well…
- Oh my God, it wasn't nice, was it?
- There are more things you can do in bed besides the plain old p in v, you know.
- I know, but here you were being all judgy, and there he was, Mr Short…
- It wasn't terrible!
- You *poor* thing.
- I still feel kinda disloyal discussing things like that.
- Why? You're done with the guy. Best time to bring forth all his inadequacies.
- It was private stuff, you know?
- You made me discuss Fat Mayank.
- Yes, but Abhi and I, we were different.
- Why? Because he was skinny?
- No! Well, yeah. I mean, we had something. We were together for a *year*.

- Semantics, darling.
- And I shouldn't have discussed Fat Mayank's thing either. That wasn't nice.
- No, it wasn't.
- I'm sorry.
- 'Sokay. He was an asshole.
- So was Abhi.
- Wow.
- What?
- That's the first time you admitted something was wrong with your precious Abhi.
- Haven't I said before?
- Nope. Definitely not. Each time I try to tell you what a jerk he was, you get all defensive.
- Do I? I hadn't noticed.
- Yes, you do. Come on, let it all out. What was his absolutely worst trait?
- I don't know.
- Yes, you do! Spill. It'll make you feel so much better.
- He…didn't like watching any movies that I liked.
- You can do much better than that.
- He cut his toenails in bed!
- Better, keep going.
- He didn't wash his underwear for *days*.
- *Now* we're getting somewhere!

- And, he was totally selfish in bed. When I got my period, it was like blow job week for him.
- You've never had period sex?
- No, I always thought it was icky.
- You're missing out on so much.
- But the blood.
- There's blood. It's sex. Things get messy. But it's still hot.
- I don't like the idea of it.
- Promise me you'll give it a shot though. With the next guy.
- If there ever *is* a next guy.
- Are we on that again?
- It's a perfectly justified fear. I'm not getting any younger, meanwhile, there are hundreds of girls turning eighteen every day, who are all clear skinned and tight bodied.
- Sometimes men like more than just firm breasts, you know.
- A) who are these men? I'd like to meet them and B) are you saying my breasts are saggy?
- You're the one who went on about eighteen-year-olds and their tight bodies.
- My breasts are *not* saggy.
- Of course they're not. You're only twenty-six.

- I did the toothbrush test on them the other day, and the toothbrush didn't stay.

- The toothbrush test?

- Yes, have you never tried it? You put your arms above your head, like this, and you put a toothbrush under your breast and if it stays, you're saggy.

- Does it have to be a toothbrush?

- No, I used a pen, but classically, *traditionally*, it's a toothbrush.

- I wonder why.

- I guess something to do with the shape? Toothbrushes have that shape, you know?

- Contoured.

- Yes, contoured! Clever girl.

- This is why you should watch more TV. Toothbrush ads are full of 'contoured' and 'bendy tops'.

- Do they actually say 'bendy tops'? Makes them sound like a sex toy.

- I think they say 'flexible heads.'

- Which is worse!

- Well, the people in the ads always look so happy, there must be a reason.

- So, do you think it says something about me that the batteries of my vibrator finish in like a week, but I charge my electric toothbrush only once every two weeks?

- Yes.
- What?
- That you need to spend less time with your vibrator and more time out in the world, for which you'll need to brush your teeth.
- My vibrator is the only man that understands me.
- Because he doesn't talk?
- Because he gets straight to the point. You know that movie *Inception?*
- The one where Leonardo DiCaprio keeps entering people's dreams?
- Yeah, and there's often another dream within the dream?
- What about it?
- Well, with my *vibrator*, it's like the *Inception* of orgasms.
- I sense you want me to ask how so, so I'll indulge you.
- Because…because, it keeps building them up and stacking them!
- Wow.
- I *know*, right?
- I need to get a vibrator.
- They're illegal in India.
- Yes, I know. I never understood why.
- Because Indian men don't like Indian women to have any pleasure.

- You are on a *roll* today!
- I had to sneak mine in from the US in my hand baggage.
- Did they see it?
- Yeah, they asked me what it was.
- What did you say?
- Well, I was holding this sparkly white thing shaped like a penis with all these fancy buttons and a remote, I said the only thing that came to me.
- Which was?
- Uncle, it's a neck massager.
- And he bought it?
- I think he was as embarrassed as I was. And the couple behind me kept giggling, so it was very hard.
- Must have been a traumatic time for you.
- Luckily, he rolled his eyes and waved me on.
- I thought it was illegal?
- I think just their sale is illegal; you can have them for your own consumption.
- Like pot.
- I'm pretty sure possessing pot is illegal too.
- Even if it's just for you?
- Even then, it's like, a *drug*, no?
- So's booze.
- Yeah, but that's legal.

- So, you're saying, if it's legal, it's allowed?
- Don't get all pot fundamentalist on me, I didn't make the rules.
- I'm just amazed you dated Abhi, who walks around in an aura of marijuana all day, like a *mushroom cloud* of grass, and didn't smoke a single joint.
- It's not my thing.
- Have you ever noticed how all your exes are pot smokers?
- Are they?
- Yes, I think you have a type.
- But I don't smoke.
- You smoke.
- I mean *smoke*-smoke.
- Ah. The old Mary Jane.
- I always thought Mary Jane was such a pretty name. It reminds me of Enid Blyton. Wasn't there a doll called Mary Jane?
- Amelia Jane.
- Amelia Jane! And she was naughty again.
- She was always naughty. Poor Amelia.
- And those oppressive toys. They never let her do what she wanted to, because she was a girl.
- Same with Famous Five. Julian and Dick used to do all the cool stuff and leave George and Ann behind because they were girls.

- I always felt for George.

- Me too! People kept telling her to be a sport or buck up or stop sulking, when really, she was just trying to establish her gender confused identity.

- You think she grew up to be a lesbian?

- Just because she was a tomboy? I don't think so. I was a tomboy.

- She wasn't *just* a tomboy though; she really, truly thought she was a boy, in a girl's body.

- Gender confusion, like I said.

- If she had been born today, she might have saved for a sex change operation.

- So, you know when boys turn into girls, they fashion them a clitoris out of the penis, right? What do they do for girls?

- I never thought about that. I guess they take some extra skin?

- Yes, but penis-as-clitoris works, because you know, they both give pleasure, but how do girls who turn into boys get boners?

- I don't think that many girls turn into boys.

- Well, I read this news story the other day, about this man who was born a woman, and he had a sex change operation, and he met a lovely woman and married her, only she couldn't have any children, so, he carried them, because they had left his uterus inside.

- *Weird.*
- I know! And you should've seen the photos, there's this guy with a beard and he's pregnant.
- Whose sperm did they use?
- Not his.
- I'm telling you, they probably don't have the equipment for it.
- All babies start out as girls though, and then after a bit, the chromosome decides whether it's an innie or an outie.
- That's why they say we're all a little bit bisexual.
- I don't know. I've never been attracted to women.
- I have.
- Really? Who?
- Oh, this girl I met at a party.
- And?
- And nothing. She was pretty, she wrapped her arms around me, we were both very drunk, and someone yelled 'kiss!' so we did.
- Oh, you were one of *those* girls.
- Which girls?
- The kind that hooks up with other girls to titillate men.
- That's a thing?
- Yes, it's a thing.

- Well, it wasn't. It was a very sweet kiss.
- Did you feel anything?
- You mean, arousal? No, not really.
- So then you weren't really attracted to her.
- I found her *attractive*.
- That's very different. I find that dog attractive. I find that bench attractive. I wouldn't necessarily have sex with either of them.
- That's a thing too.
- Dog and bench threesomes?
- Hah. No. People who find objects attractive. There was a woman who married the Eiffel Tower.
- Oh, I think I read about that. And another woman who loved a fence.
- I don't think that's true.
- It is! I read it! She took the fence home and shared a bed with it and everything.
- You are so making this up.
- You're being size-ist again. You can imagine someone marrying the Eiffel Tower but not a fence?
- I can *understand* someone marrying the Eiffel Tower, it's gorgeous, it's a symbol and in your head, you know you're not really married to it, but what it represents to you.
- A fence could be just as sexy as the Eiffel Tower.

- Is this about Fat Mayank again?
- I'm just saying. A fence requires a lot of architecture. All that wood, and how you stack it, and there are so many different kinds of fences. It may not be the *Eiffel Tower*, but however humble, it has beauty.
- Look, I'm sure Fat Mayank was a lovely boyfriend.
- This is not about Fat Mayank! This is about how you need to learn to accept that other things, things that don't match the grand ideal in your head about What Stuff Should Look Like, For You To Fall In Love With It, also exist.
- Wow.
- I'm sorry, it just needed to be said.
- I could *feel* the capital letters in that sentence.
- Well, I was imagining them too.
- Do I do that?
- Of course you do! You have these impossible ideals, oh my perfect boyfriend will look like something out of a magazine ad, he will do the crossword with me and we will have a Labrador and go boating!
- Okay, first of all, I get seasick, and second of all, what's wrong with someone wanting to do the crossword?
- Nothing. Nothing's wrong with that, it's just that you have this checklist, and everything has to be marked off against that.
- No, I don't.

- Yes, you do! You know what? You already have someone to do the crossword with: me. You have someone to go drinking with, you have someone to share your love of sappy romance novels, they just don't all have to be the same person.

- But what is the point of a boyfriend if he isn't everything you want?

- There you go again. There is no 'point'.

- I hate it when you make air quotes at me.

- A boyfriend is not meant to have a 'point' and I'll air quote if I want to—he's meant to be someone you like and someone you enjoy spending time with. Period.

- You're saying you should marry someone even if you have nothing in common with them?

- I'm saying you should marry someone. Actually, I never used the word 'marriage', but still; if they make you happy. Even if they don't like doing the crossword and Labradors trigger off their asthma. Even if they're a fence and you thought you'd be with an Eiffel Tower.

- That's quite beautiful.

- Are you still ignoring my point?

- No, no, your point's been taken, I'm thinking about it.

- Well, there was Dushyant. Your boyfriend before Abhi.

- Ugh, Dush*yant*.

- Precisely. The guy was a walking turd. And yet, you hung on to him for three years.

its a vulgar slang. a person regarded as obnoxious

- I thought I loved him. —

- Did you? Did you really?

- Well, in bits, he was sweet.

- What bits would that be? The bits when he got super drunk and yelled at you? The bits where he was mean to waiters and household help?

- That should've tipped me off.

- I'll say. You can tell a lot about a guy by how he treats people who serve him.

- But none of you said anything!

- We tried. We really did try. But you know how you get when you like someone. You dig your heels in and refuse to listen.

- I do not!

- It was the same with Abhi. He cheated on you, Maya! Twice! And you just kept taking him back.

- He promised he would change.

- They never change. Once a cheater, always a cheater.

- There are many people who have one-off affairs, regret them and go back to living a happy life with their partners.

- Fair enough. I'm sure those people exist. But Abhi wasn't one of them.

- He said he was sorry. He cried, even.

- And then he just went back out and did it again. You know, I have a theory.

- Do I want to hear this theory?

- You might learn something, it's a pretty good theory.

- Okay.

- I believe that the people who are cheated on keep taking back the person who cheated on them because of the way they act immediately after they've been found out.

- What do you mean?

- I mean, like as soon as you discovered Abhi was cheating, and there were all these tears and remorse and stuff, didn't he act extra sweet? *deep* *regret*

- Yes, I suppose.

- He bought you flowers, he showered you with attention.

- We went on a getaway to the hills.

- Exactly. It was like you had first started dating. The honeymoon period all over again.

- So, you're saying I took him back just because I liked that feeling?

- Oh, I don't think you did it consciously. But it's hard to keep up the honeymoon period in any relationship. It's like, addictive, you know? When you're always leaping for your phone, when you realise that they're the first person you think of when you wake up and the last when you go to sleep, the fluttery feelings. You know what I mean.

- It *was* nice.
- I can bet it was nice. And no one can blame you for wanting more of that. Which is why maybe you took him back the second time.
- Oh, I'm so *stupid*!
- Oh babe, you're not stupid. You're human. It's normal. He was a jerk of a boyfriend, so it was surprisingly pleasant when he was nice to you.
- I broke up with him before he cheated on me the third time though. Nush? Nush! What is it?
- I didn't want to have to be the one to tell you.
- He did it again, didn't he?
- I'm really sorry, Maya.
- He was cheating on me, a third time.
- He's an asshole!
- Who was it this time?
- Is that really important?
- I'd like to know. Call it closure.
- Tanvi.
- Tanvi. Not Tanvi-the-slut?
- Yeah.
- So, he went back to her.
- I guess.

- And now they're dating?

- I'm not sure of the details, but that's what it seems like.

- Wow.

- More fool her though, right? Look at you, so much better off out of it.

- I thought the cheating boyfriend never left his girlfriend for the other woman. That's what you hear everywhere.

- Well, he might have never left you. You dumped him, after all.

- And now he's with her. I really am the Universe's Stepdaughter.

- *I* love you.

- I wish I could do something drastic, you know? Like egg her house, or give his car a flat tyre.

- What would be the point? *violent anger*   *unworthy*

- I don't know. Hell hath no fury like a woman scorned and all that.   *feeling*

- You'd just make yourself look like the psycho chick. They'd be all cozy inside—

- Don't!

- I'm sorry! They'd be plotting evil things, and he'd have a zit and she's fat and they'd be all, 'Oh my God, Maya is a psycho, you're so much better off without her.'

- We don't want them to think that.

- No. We want him to come crawling to you, on his knees, and say, 'I don't know what I was thinking.'
- And I'll slam the door on his face?
- And you'll slam the door on his face. Not before saying, 'That's because you never know what you're thinking, you stupid jerk!'
- I'm sure I could come up with a better insult than jerk.
- I'm sure you could. I'm just giving you a template here. Feel free to mess around with it.
- Sooo.
- Yes.
- Speaking of jumping to check their phones every couple of minutes, guess which of the two of us has been doing that all afternoon? I'll give you a hint. It's not me.
- Why, whatever do you mean?
- Don't act coy with me, missy. Either you're doing that Eiffel Tower thing where you're suddenly attracted to your phone, or, could it be possible that someone on the other end is making your heart go patter-pit?
- Maya!
- Let's see, what could your phone password be? Let's try your birthday.
- Give. Me. My. Phone. Now.

- Wait, grabby! Have some patience. Ah, here we are. Text messages.

- Ma-*ya*.

- Nooooooo!

- It's really rude to read someone's messages.

- Tell me it's not true!

- I don't know what you're talking about.

- You're not starting a romance between you and Hiten Ahluwalia?

- I, we, we message every now and then.

- Hiten though. *My* Hiten. The Hiten whose penis we were just discussing?

- Well, technically he's not really *your* Hiten anymore, is he?

- He was *my* boyfriend. Farad was yours. Didn't we just review that?

- Like decades ago!

- So what is his penis like, then, hmmm?

- I refuse to talk about this anymore.

- Why? You were perfectly happy to a little while ago. What's changed?

- I was going to tell you.

- Yeah, about that. Why didn't you?

- I thought you'd be mad.

- Do I look mad?

- A little bit, yeah.
- I'm not mad. At least, I'm not mad that it's Hiten and you. I'm mad that you didn't tell me.
- I just thought. You have so many things.
- You keep doing this. You don't have to keep protecting me. It's fine. I'm your friend. I want to hear about you in Fat Mayank's T-shirt eating Maggi. I want to hear that Abhi is dating Tanvi. And most importantly, if you've found someone new, I want to hear all about it from beginning to end.
- I didn't want to be all happy when you weren't.
- But, the fact that you're happy, it's like the best news I've gotten all day.
- It isn't anything yet though.
- How did it start?
- How else? Facebook. He added me, we got talking.
- He doesn't live in Bombay?
- No, he's based out of Singapore now.
- I guess you could commute.
- You're getting ahead of yourself. It's not even at that stage yet.
- You're totally blushing! What stage is it in?
- We talk a lot. On the phone. He calls, randomly.
- Email?
- Lots of email.

- Phone sex?

- Maya!

- Just asking.

- No phone sex. But.

- Yes?

- But he's here next week.

- Is he flying in just for you?

- Sort of, he also has work, which means he gets a hotel.

- A hotel! Oooh!

- Shuttup. Stop making fun of me.

- I'm not. I'm actually, genuinely thrilled.

- Obviously, since we haven't seen each other in like ten years, we're going to have to take things slow.

- So, you don't know what he looks like?

- I sort of do, because of Skype and his photos online, but not like the complete picture.

- I always thought he was cute.

- Well, I'm glad he won't get a weird nickname.

- No, not Hiten. He's always been one of my favourite boyfriends.

- That's so weird when you say it like that.

- We *were* dating. But nothing as sexy as a hotel room. He only grabbed my boob once.

- You said.

- During *The Matrix*.

- You said.
- It was a nice boob grab. Sort of friendly. Not all aggressive, like some men are.
- I'm really not interested.
- Of course you are. Don't lie. And he was a good kisser too, not like Octopus.
- He got married.
- Who? Octopus? To the neighbour girl?
- No, not to the neighbour girl, what are we, in a Hindi movie?
- Today seems a bit Hindi movie-esque. ~~in the style of resembling~~
- He had an arranged marriage, like a good boy.
- Did Hiten go to the wedding?
- No, it seems they've sort of lost touch over the years.
- Boys.
- I know. He was really surprised to hear you and I were still friends.
- Why wouldn't we be? Did he say nice things about me?
- He said he remembered you fondly.
- And?
- He didn't say anything about your boob, if that's what you're asking.
- I would have thought my boob went down in the golden hall of boob touching for him.

- You know he likes me, right?
- So?
- So, he's not going to bring up your boob, golden or not.
- But now you're going to think about it when he touches yours.
- Dammit!
- Sor-*ree.* They are quite golden though. Want to touch?
- No, thanks. I'm good.
- So, you and Hiten.
- Is this going to be your only topic of conversation now?
- You have to admit, it's very romantic. At your wedding, when I give a toast, I'll be all like, 'I met him only so Nush could marry him.'
- We don't have toasts at Indian weddings.
- Pity. We should. When you and Hiten get married, we'll have a toast.
- Not if you're giving it.
- What's wrong with my toasts? I'd give a great toast.
- You'd talk about his grabbing your boob.
- It was quite a turning point for me, I'll admit. A sort of coming of age. But no, I won't say anything about boob grabbing. I'll talk about this.
- This?

- This. This afternoon. Golden sunlight on a rainy day. Us. How we were thinking about all the men that were in our lives before, oh, I guess I'll have to edit that part a little; don't want your in-laws thinking you're a slut, okay, how we were talking of days gone by, and we had lost hope.
- You lost hope.
- So did you! I thought you'd never date again after Fat Mayank.
- Anyway, go on.
- I thought you didn't want my toast.
- I'm getting drawn into it against my will.
- Sure you are. It's a fantastic toast. Anyway, so, yeah, here we were, friends from back in the day, and how sometimes, if you look carefully, friends from back in the day can be what you need in the future too.
- Huh.
- And then I'll toss in some stuff about the Eiffel Tower and the fence, because that bit was pretty cool.
- Thanks, I try.
- I should go home now.
- Hey, we forgot about fixing your tattoo.
- I'll do it tomorrow. Can you at least read what it says?
- Yup. Clear as day. Looks a bit better than it did in the beginning. Look, now that the swelling's gone down, see, there's space for a carrot.

- A caret, you mean.
- I like your way better.
- Nush?
- Hmm?
- You will tell me if I got the description of his penis right, right?
- Not in a million years.
- Nush!
- Maya.
- Oh, alright. At least tell him I said hello. And send him a picture of the tattoo. He might appreciate it.
- I just did, but the picture quality isn't great.
- Oh. Well, tell him what it says.
- I'm typing it. See? 'Well behved women seldom make history.'
- What did he say?
- He said, 'Is there an 'a' missing?'
- Tell him about the carrots.
- Okay.

৪৩

THE ENGLISH TEACHER

DURJOY DATTA

Since time immemorial, English teachers in Indian schools have been the subject of erotic fantasies of hundreds of hormonally charged students, even as they explain without success why two past tenses can't be used in a single sentence. Kunal Roy was no different. As his English teacher, Mrs Ravina Sharma, bent over to pick the answer sheets from the rickety table in front of her, all his eyes could see was her succulent bosom staring right at his face, he was filled to his brim in primal, sexual energy. Clad in a saree that clung to her body, accentuating her generous assets, she pulled the rubber band off the stack of answer sheets and straightened them.

Behind Kunal's short cropped hair and thick skull, the class was empty. He was perched precariously over Mrs Ravina on the teacher's desk and was going at her breasts with unmatched ferocity, his football-hardened body chafing against the porcelain smooth skin of his English teacher, six years his senior and married. Kunal had a strange fascination towards newly married women. He thought they give off an obvious sexual vibe, maybe because they are in the most sexual part of their lives. They radiate it, they smell of it, and they look like they did it just moments ago. The glowing skin, the excessive make-up, the desire to be a good wife, gives them a hallowed space in the darkest areas of men's fantasies. The thought of newly married women always gave him an adrenaline rush.

Kunal had never been a teacher's pet, even though he had always been an above average student who kept his nosy, academically inclined parents more than happy. He was too sweaty, too rough, and too sportsman-like to hang around staff rooms while inside, the teachers discussed the latest issues of glossy female magazines, the effects aging was having on certain body parts, and their husbands' waning interests in them. But Kunal knew Mrs Ravina was different. She was young, and had just completed her M.Phil in English literature a few years back. She was younger than the rest of his teachers—a fact supported by her perky breasts and taut skin over her high cheekbones—and didn't look the type who would aim for the gossip queen title amongst teachers. Moreover, she was just an ad hoc teacher who could be asked to leave whenever the old, permanent, teacher joined back after her maternity leave.

Mrs Ravina distributed the answer sheets, her slender hands in constant motion. Her parted lips read out the names on the answer sheets and smiled to acknowledge the good performances in the class. Kunal Roy's performance had dipped further and it became clear that he would have to give at least a few improvement tests before the board examinations. A cleverly executed plan.

'Kunal,' she said, 'meet me after the lunch break in the staff room.' She looked away and praised students who had managed to reproduce what they had mugged with Yoda-like efficiency the night before the exam, on the answer sheets. But Kunal Roy was smiling the widest, much like the famous stammering Indian superstar who said, 'To lose is to win' or something like that.

'She is so sweet, isn't she? I wish I could have her forever,' Kunal said to his desk partner, who was busy gloating about the totalling mistake in his answer sheet.

৪০৫৫

The coaches were thinking of retiring Kunal Roy's jersey number next year as a mark of respect to the laurels he had brought to the school in the last five years. It was his last year on the football field and he had done more for the game than the whole team combined. As a puny eighth grader, he had single-handedly powered the team to seven straight victories in the championship and ended the preoccupation of the school with cricket, along with the jock-status of the cricketers. He, alone, was responsible for the now vibrant sex life of every new entrant in the football team.

But that day, things were different. What would have been three easy goals had ended up warming up opposing team's goalie's padded gloves. He was clearly distracted, his mind elsewhere. Every few seconds, he would check his watch, counting seconds backwards to the time he would be alone in a closed space with Mrs Ravina, only a yard separating his heaving body from hers. It was high time. For the last month, starting from exactly three days after Mrs Ravina had joined, Kunal had followed her everywhere.

'Bad game, skip,' the goalie of Kunal's team said, as he went past him. He didn't mind; he had bigger things to worry about. After packing his sports gear, but still in his sullied football uniform, he walked in to the men's washroom closest to her staff room. Shirtless, he studied himself in the mirror. He didn't look seventeen. The previous year, in the game against the Salwan Boys, a referee had called foul play thinking Kunal was a local club player, not a student, and a lot older than the seventeen years he claimed on the fact sheet.

He wiped the sweat off his body and stood there, admiring the muscle he had gained in the past few years. Still no match for his hunky, model-like classmates who were regulars at the school gym, but none of them had abs as well defined as his. He put his football T-shirt on, having seen in numerous 'My First Sex Teacher' porn that students who played sports were often the subject of a dark fantasy of strict-teachers-with-horn-rimmed-glasses.

He fought with the streaming images in his head; images of Mrs Ravina's long, wavy black hair grasped firmly in his hands, as hers crept up his nylon football shorts to spring his manhood free, and of her playful eyelashes batting while she flirts coquettishly with his member down south. Knocking those images out of his head, and after spraying himself with copious quantities of deodorant, he walked out of the washroom.

The sweat came screaming down his temple as he flitted nervously outside the staff room. With trembling hands, he knocked on the door and asked, 'May I come in?'

'Yes, come in,' the sugary voice from the other side said.

'Good afternoon, ma'am,' he stammered as his eyes met Mrs Ravina's big almond shaped brown eyes. Her smooth, shiny, flat-as-a-washboard stomach lay in full view and he struggled to tear his eyes off it.

'Sit,' she said and pointed to a chair. He felt the blood rush downwards.

'Thank you.'

'Kunal, you know why I have called you, don't you? Your performance has been steadily dipping. At the beginning of the year, you were one of the highest scorers and now you're finding it difficult to even pass your exams? What's the problem?' she asked.

This is going well, he thought. In the porn movies he had

watched, it all started with a problem and ended in animal grunts, moans, rhythmic pelvic thrusts, cries to go harder, and the teacher's promise that sex will go on secretly in abandoned classrooms and stuffy washrooms.

'I have been distracted. With the football practice and...' he paused.

'And *me*?' she asked, batting her eyelids rather unnaturally.

'Umm...yes, ma'am.'

'Tell me about it,' she said, arching forward, the tiny cleavage beneath the blue saree spiked a surge in testosterone in his body, giving him sexual gooseflesh. *This is going perfect!* 'Am I not a good teacher?' she asked, chewing the pencil in her hand, biting it and almost suckling on it. 'The other teachers say so. They say I am not good enough.' She swirled the pencil in her mouth, her tongue wrapped around the rubber end of it, making it wet. Her lips were parted wide open, her hands brushing against the side of her soft mounds. The sight of her fingers, long and slender, sent him into throes of frenzy, as he imagined her nails scratching against his body.

'Your teaching skills are par excellence,' he assured her. He figured the other teachers were just jealous, as she was someone their potbellied husbands would fancy them turning into during the last mile of their pathetic, monotonous, missionary style orgasms. She was what they imagined themselves to be, and wished they could be. Their criticism was nothing but cleverly concealed soap opera jealousy, reserved for younger sisters-in-law with glowing skins and gravity defying breasts.

'Then what's bothering you?' she queried, leaning over more, her bosom inches away from him.

'I can't help...but fantasise about you. You're all I think about, ma'am. Ever since I saw you, I have followed you everywhere. You live in Gangotri Apartments, opposite to the MCD School. You wake up at six thirty every morning and go for a morning walk at the DDA Park nearby. Mostly, you wear your pink track pants and a black razor back. Sometimes, your husband accompanies you. He has a small business of spare parts in Chandni Chowk. The lights go out at twelve every night...' he said. His voice trailed off before he could tell her how he had climbed up the drain pipe in an unsuccessful attempt to place a spy cam he had bought off the internet in her bedroom. Before he could tell her that he had spent sleepless nights thinking about her, that he had once bought movie tickets close of their seats and had felt like killing himself on seeing her face buried in her husband's shoulder. There were times when he felt murderous seeing her husband wrap himself around her. The urge was not to see him vanish, but to see him suffer, to make him pay for every time he had touched Mrs Ravina. But he stopped himself before he could tell her that.

Blood rushed to his face, his palms started to sweat and he started to look everywhere but at her. He readied himself for an onslaught of harsh words for his perversion, and was caught off-guard when he felt her hands grasp his shoulder. He blanked out and felt out of breath as he felt her body against his. Her heaving breasts strafed against his chest and he struggled for air. Her lips hovered around his ears and he could feel her warm breath. Her tongue snaked to his earlobe and sent jitters down his spine. Trembling, he put his hands around her tiny waist. The feeling of her naked skin in his hands felt like an out of body experience. All the years of deprivation accumulated in that single moment as he grew inside his pants. Beads of sweat rolled down his forehead on to his nose and he looked at the growing bump in his nylon shorts. She followed his eyes to the bump and met his gaze, her eyes wide and wielding an inexplicable expression.

'Close the door,' she said, her voice suddenly husky.

He got up with a start, almost as a reflex and bolted towards the door. He latched it shut. Mrs Ravina giggled and in a second, her lips parted and her demeanour changed to sexy as she leaned far back into her chair. Kunal's entire pornographic history flashed in front of his eyes.

'Come here,' she said. 'Why are you looking at me like that? What's going on? Kunal? Are you okay? Kunal Roy!'

The sound finally registered. He snapped out of his fantasy. He was still outside the staff room.

ೞೞ

Kunal sat at the last bench of his classroom, absentmindedly doodling on the last page of his notebook. His thoughts were where they always were. He had no idea how to control them, and he did not even want to try. He was happy when he thought about her. Just thinking about her made him feel warm inside, and he was not willing to let go of that feeling. He was obsessed, the magnitude of which was increasing by the minute.

The bell rang, announcing the end of math period. A shiver went down his spine. *Math period was followed by English.* He had seen Mrs Ravina in the morning at the school assembly (and three more times as he purposefully passed by her classes—he obviously had her schedule saved in his head—on pretence of going to the toilet). She was wearing a yellow saree, with a contrasting neon pink blouse. Ah, that blouse.

His eyes fixed intently at the door, he felt his breath grow heavy in anticipation. And when she finally entered the classroom, his palms started sweating. He wiped them on his trousers, as the class rose to greet their teacher.

'Good morning! Sit, sit,' she said cheerfully, unloading a stack of textbooks she was carrying with her on her desk. 'So, how are we doing today?'

She was like that—always cheerful—a smile constantly on her lips. Except in his imagination...there, her lips didn't just smile. She opened up the English textbook and picked up from where she had left the previous day. As if by magic, the class settled down. There was pin-drop silence whenever she was teaching; she was the kind of woman who when entered a room, everyone sat up and noticed. That's the kind of attention she commanded when she walked into a room with a purpose.

As she walked across the classroom, speaking, he concentrated on her lips moving. The bright pink lipstick went with her blouse. The colour looked prettier against her pearly white teeth when she spoke. She was wearing a nose ring that day—not very big—barely big enough to catch one's attention though. And his attention was caught. She came by his row and was just about to pass him by when his eyes closed. He had not intended to close them; they seemed to have a mind of their own. He had stopped looking at her. His head was bent down, his eyes shut, his nostrils inhaling the sweet smell of her perfume... mixed with the smell of *her*.

He knew what her perfume smelt like; he had a bottle of the same at home. But it was never the same when he sprayed some to try and capture her smell. It was the perfume mixed with her natural scent, which created a heady mixture that never failed to get him intoxicated. He inhaled deeply, as the *pallu* of her saree brushed past his hand. Without meaning to, he held it.

She stopped walking and turned around, to check where her *pallu* got stuck. 'What are you doing?' she asked.

Kunal opened his eyes abruptly and looked up at her. She was looking at him, only him, all of her focus on him—his breath caught when he realised that.

'Kunal?' she said.

He stammered, 'Yes...yes ma'am?' He quickly let go of the end of her pallu and said, 'My...my ring...your saree...got caught...'

'No, but why aren't you taking this down?' she asked.

'Huh?'

He looked around the classroom to find that while he had been busy staring at his teacher, the rest of his classmates had their notebooks out on their desks and were jotting down what Mrs Ravina had apparently been dictating. He stood up slowly.

'Answer me.'

'Ma'am, I...I...'

'Yes?' she prodded, now looking a little concerned. 'Is everything okay?'

Kunal was finding it difficult to form words and shove them out of his mouth. He would rather just stare at her— there was nothing better. Or maybe there was, but all *that* happened only in his imagination. He forced himself to look away from her, and down at his desk.

'Answer me,' Mrs Ravina said sternly.

'I am sorry.'

'What do you mean you are sorry? I am asking you why you are not taking this down. I need a reason from you, not a vague apology. Is this not important enough for you?'

'It is, ma'am,' Kunal said hurriedly. 'I just...didn't have a pen.'

'What rubbish! You could not have asked anyone for a pen? Where's your notebook? And your textbook? You don't have those either?'

'I do.'

As he dug into his bag to pull out his notebook, Mrs Ravina shook her head in frustration. 'I am teaching here... Were you even listening?'

'Yes, ma'am.'

'Great, so tell me what we were discussing.'

Kunal stared at her for a brief moment before forcing himself to look down at his clammy hands.

'Do you even know which chapter we are at?'

'Umm...' He did not have the faintest idea.

Mrs Ravina sighed. 'I don't understand what is wrong with you. You were just sitting there blankly, doing...what? What were you doing?'

Looking at you.

'What?'

He looked up at her in horror.

'What did you just say?' she lowered her voice and repeated.

He hadn't realised he had said it out loud. They looked at each other, and kept looking. He could see that she was mad at him. Her eyebrows were crumpled and her eyes squinting slightly, as they pierced into his. After a moment, she stepped closer to him.

'I am your teacher. Weren't you taught to respect your elders?' she muttered through clenched teeth.

He kept looking into her eyes, which were furious.

'Answer me. Why aren't you saying anything? You are really disturbing me. Kunal, I think I will need to ask your parents to come in for a sit-down.'

He gulped.

'And stop looking at me like that! This is all very unsettling.'

And unsettled she looked. Her expressions had changed from fury to confusion, concern and a certain amount of... *fear*, was it?

'Get out,' Mrs Ravina said and stepped back.

He didn't move an inch.

'Get out of my class,' she said louder, so that the whole class could hear. 'And ask your parents to find time to meet me tomorrow. I'll have admin give them a call too.'

Finally, he looked away from her, slid out from behind his desk and walked towards the door, a crooked smile spreading across his face. He stepped out of the classroom and stood by the door, leaning against the wall. His smile was getting wider and wider. He did not mind not being in the class and not being able to see her, even. He had enough mental images to last him the day. He was oddly excited about what had happened. It was the longest one-on-one conversation they had had since their association with each other as teacher and student. Somehow, it was even better than everything he had imagined in his head all this time. This was *her*, the real her; not a figment of his imagination. She could think, speak and act on her own, in her own way, without Kunal having to decide these for her.

He replayed the incident in his head. He replayed her facial expressions—from confusion to concern, to fury, to confusion and concern again, and just a tad of fear at one point. It did something to him—the mixture of fury and fear in her face.

It turned him on.

ༀ

Days passed by and Kunal was listless about how to control his growing obsession with her. He knew he had to manage his rising urges. He went a week without fantasising about her in his morning showers. But then, when he gave in, he did it nineteen times in a single day. His condition worsened as he found himself stationed outside her house 24/7. Often, it felt as if someone else controlled his body and his actions. Sometimes, he realised he had no recollection of how he got to stone hard benches of the park she used to go to for her morning walks. His extreme dislike for Mrs Ravina's husband grew exponentially. Their love seemed to strengthen with time, the hugs became longer, the kisses now seemed more out of love than rabid lust, and they took out more time to experience the little joys of life together.

The boards came and went. He did well in all the subjects barring English, which he barely passed. Luckily, he got through a government engineering college. Without a second thought, he shifted to a hostel and chalked out an elaborate schedule to track Mrs Ravina's whereabouts. His fantasies, which earlier were based out of Mills & Boon books—naked, passionate and gratifying, were now more about domination and kink. In his dreams, he could see her lying helplessly on her back, bound in chains and submitting to all his desires. The more he saw the love between the married couple blossom, the more violent his dreams became. Her husband became a common feature in his dreams. Often, he imagined him being in relentless pain, knowing that his wife was wilfully yielding to another man's wishes.

As his first semester examinations approached, his frenzied watch on Mrs Ravina intensified. From the earnings of a few home tuitions he had taken up, he rented a miniscule flat close to her apartment. Later, he got himself a pair of binoculars. When just watching her from a distance wasn't enough for him to gratify himself, he started recording her and watching the tapes over and over again. He used to cut and edit the clips of videos to make it look like she was entering his apartment, and not hers. For some reason unknown to him, he started to stock things you would find in a serial killer's hideout. Knives. Chains. Ropes. Between all these contraptions, sometimes he scared even himself.

Slowly, his attendance started to dip. The professors got concerned about the classes he missed and the frequent fights he got into. His aggression often startled people. It was like the onset of a second puberty. The only time he was calm was when he watched her. The people in his building loved him. He taught their kids and was well mannered. Though they had no idea of what went on in his perverse head.

He wasn't allowed to sit for his second semester exams. On being caught with notes stashed down his underwear, he had lashed out at the invigilator and broken his nose. He was lucky not to have been suspended. That day, he went back to his dingy apartment, feeling lost and angry. Rage dominated psychological profile. *Something needs to be done*, he thought. *I need to get over her*, he reprimanded himself. *Or find a way out...*

৯০৫৫

Kunal Roy was smiling the widest at the Annual Excellence Awards at his company. For the third year in a row, he was adjudged as one of the star employees of the South Asia wing of the company. He spearheaded most of the innovative projects of the R&D department in India, of the Norwegian cell phone company. Not only was he respected for his ideas, but revered for his ideals. He had completed all his education from Delhi, rejecting generous offers from universities across the better parts of the world. If anything, he was the glowing example of how your college doesn't play a part in your success, a case in point against brain drain.

By the time the evening came to an end, he was exhausted. The smiles, the thank-yous, the handshakes, and the small talk took a toll on him. He had hardly got any time to eat. The raging hunger didn't allow him to wait any longer. Just as he turned to walk towards the buffet, he spotted someone who made his heart wobble. A woman—newlywed—was sitting at a distance, her long legs crossed, and her eyes roving restlessly around the banquet hall. She was waiting for somebody. Her face looked strangely familiar, like a face from the past. In that second, he felt transported back to his school days when he used to obsess over a woman who looked almost exactly like this woman across the hall. No matter how hard he tried, he couldn't look away. The woman's long hair flirted with her eyes and she kept swatting it away. She kept nibbling at her food and it seemed like she did so more out of boredom than anything else. Kunal Roy's eyes didn't blink. He was staring at his past, once again. His heart, his mind started chugging like an old coal locomotive fired after decades of neglect. The images were rusty at first, then they became clearer, and he could finally see clearly. The woman looked freakishly like Mrs Ravina. The face of the young woman in front of him seared itself on his temporal lobe, almost obliterating the previous face.

Moments later, the husband appeared and the woman broke into an enrapturing smile. They hugged. The rage came back to him. Suddenly, he was furious. He closed his eyes and took a few long breaths. He did not want to think about the woman anymore. And he definitely did not want to follow her into her car. Or take a picture from his cell phone.

He couldn't eat. But the sandwiches begged to be tasted. Hurriedly, he wrapped a few in a tissue paper. He left the building and headed home. Despite numerous requests, he had not shifted out from the apartment he had rented in his college days. Ten years... He argued that he was emotionally attached to it. Moreover, he wasn't married, so there was no need for him to shift into a bigger apartment. On his way to his home, a few neighbours smiled at him and he smiled back. They knew him as a gentle, nice boy.

He unlocked the door. Almost immediately, his lips curved into a smile. He switched on the light. The place was just like it was ten years ago. Not a thing had changed. At the corner, there were the chains he had bought when he was in college. Shackled in those chains was a woman who had been missing for ten years now.

'Ravina ma'am, are you hungry? I got you some food,' Kunal smiled.

The woman cowered.

Kunal walked towards her with the sandwiches, smiling, oblivious to the fact that the police had finally pinpointed the abductor and were about to knock on his door in less than a minute.

ॐ

THE RETURN OF THE (ORIGINAL) VAMPIRE

JUDY BALAN

I met a girl last night. No, it's not like that. I know everyone says that, but I need you to understand that it *really* is not like that. See, I'm new to this city, so I decided to get out last night and get a real taste of it. You know, *literally*. But the strangest thing happened. As a result of which, I found myself at the shrink's office first thing in the morning, battling identity issues. Well, that was before the quack diagnosed me as a delusional psychopath of some kind. Bipolar, schizophrenic—one of those things. And had me bound, injected me with all sorts of pointless sedatives (that don't work on my species), put a TV remote in my hand and…no, I won't ruin the ending for you.

'So, how long have you felt this compulsive need to rip open carotid arteries and feed on people's blood?' Dr Quack said.

'Uhh, ever since I became a vampire?' I said. He looked at me with curiosity and a discouraging level of fearlessness. This wasn't supposed to go this way. I was here to find myself, not have my whole existence questioned.

'And when did that happen?' he finally asked me, being careful not to break his penetrating gaze. Because, you know, *that's* what it takes to get to a vampire.

'Since Count Dracula bit me, of course,' I said. He didn't laugh. Instead, he took notes. Was he kidding?

'Uhh, that was a joke,' I said. 'Of course I'm aware that Dracula is entirely fictional.'

Now I really had his attention. I could almost read his thoughts—*delusional vampire patient laughs at the suggestion of Dracula being real.* Well, more or less. With a few jargons thrown in. He leaned forward, about to say something, but I wasn't in the mood to indulge his sad, limited paradigm. I could have just pounced on him and demonstrated the validity of my existence but it was too easy. And again, I wasn't in the mood.

'No!' I said before he could get a word out. This is *my* time and I get to do the talking.'

'Please,' he said, gesturing for me to start talking. I knew it was pointless, but I needed to tell somebody about the weirdest night of my life and a shrink seemed sensible as 'somebodies' went. But now that I think about it, the whole idea seems kind of dumb. Which is particularly depressing considering I'm having all these identity issues. I mean, you go through your whole life believing you're someone and out of the blue, you're made to question all of it. By some silly, deluded *girl* at that.

I sighed dramatically. 'Where do I begin?' I said. More to myself, but Dr Quack chose to give me direction.

'Start with the time you turned into a vampire,' he said.

I snorted. 'Uhh, no. This is about last night. I met a girl.'

I barely started to speak and he went, 'Oh, so this is a relationship issue!' He sounded relieved. What an idiot. Were therapists even supposed to interrupt so much?

'No!' I said. Firmly, this time. He leaned back on his chair, finally letting me get to the story.

'It was past midnight and I was walking the pathway behind Smoky Joe's Pizza.'

I was barely into my first sentence when he interrupted. 'You mean, Smokin' Joe's,' he said. You see what I mean now? Was this really essential?

I ignored him and continued. 'I had found my target. She was pretty, self-involved, distracted by shiny objects and couldn't be more than twenty-two. A vampire couldn't ask for more.'

'And why is that?' the Quack wanted to know.

'Well, for starters, they're easy prey. It's so much easier to lure a girl into the dark when she's busy texting, entirely unaware of the fact that you've been following her for the last twenty minutes. But that's not even the best part. You see, we're predators and we enjoy the hunt. And airheads are our favourite brand. They're shrill, terrified and adorable as hell when they try to outrun you. It's just the rush we seek when we're on a hunt.' I expected Dr Quack to interject with an ignorant observation about vampirism but he refrained. In fact, I think at this point, he had got too caught up in the story—willing suspension of disbelief and all that.

'So I stalked her, slowly worked my way to the point where she noticed me lurking in the shadows and then that piercing scream when I finally went for her,' I sighed dramatically, reliving the rush of the moment. 'Man, I thought I really had her.'

'And then?' Quack said.

'And then, the strangest thing happened. I held her by the head, went for her neck, and instead of freaking out about what kind of monster she was dealing with, she immediately figured out that I was a vampire.' At this point, I paused and looked at the Quack. 'She was smarter than you,' I said.

The Quack didn't care. He was too engrossed in the story. 'And? What happened?' he said.

'And,' I said, 'she seemed excited to see me.'

'What? Why?'

'That's kind of what you're supposed to be helping me with.'

'Well, go on. What happened next? Did you attack her?'

'No. I mean, I didn't want to!'

'You liked her?' he asked me. What's up with this human need to believe in true love against all odds!

'God, no! Are you even listening to me? This woman *weirded* me out!'

'Okay, okay—tell me the whole story.'

'Nope, I can't,' I said. I'm already out of time and I can't afford another session with you.'

'What if *I* paid you to tell me?'

I smiled, for the first time since the incident. 'Well that changes everything.'

So we ordered the pizza (from Smokin' Joe's), Dr Quack cancelled the rest of his appointments for the day and I began my story.

ఇంలు

'Oh, my God! Oh, my God!' she made a cackling sound. 'You're a vampire! Are you for real? Oh my God!' As you might imagine, I wasn't prepared for that. She was actually jumping up and down like a five-year-old on a sugar rush.

I stepped back. She probably thought I was an idiot in a Halloween costume. So I put on my most menacing voice. 'Huh? I am not in a Halloween costume and you are about to have the worst night of your life.' I expected her to scream, of course. Or try to fight back. Or my favourite— run. And yet, she was still there. Saying things.

'Oh, that's what they always say!' she said in that

excruciatingly shrill voice that makes my fangs go back inside. 'Oh! Are those your fangs?' she said, as if on cue. 'Can I touch them? Please?'

I took it all in and in one grand attempt to outdo her, I made my Scary Predator sound. It's a sound I have rehearsed for the most extreme of circumstances but have never actually had to use. Until now. So I let out my most terrifying sound and went for her neck once again and you know what she said? 'Ooh, that's it, that's it. Bite me!' And she made an orgasmic face to go with it. You know? Just in case, I hadn't felt *completely* emasculated. Er, *evampulated*, already.

'What the fuck's wrong with you?' I asked.

'What the fuck's wrong with *you*? Why won't you bite me?'

'Why aren't you running for your life?'

'Because I've been dreaming about meeting a vampire for the last three years!'

I had to admit, she had me. 'What? Why?' I asked.

'Because I'm a romantic, looking for my epic love and this,' she pointed to some invisible non-chemistry between us, 'is just meant to be. I know it!'

Perhaps intimidation was the wrong way to go, I conceded. Besides, I had to find out just what kind of rubbish vampire theories were doing the rounds on the streets, before I set out on the next big hunt. Maybe she could be my asset in the real world. The one who gives me inside information. What? I've watched Homeland.

'And what on earth could have possibly given you that idea?' I asked, genuinely curious. 'Besides, aren't all the girls looking for that Mr Darcy guy?'

She snorted and started walking, holding my hand and dreamily smiling at the moon. I indulged her, though it made the skin on the back of my neck crawl all the way up to my head. I needed to know just what the hell was going on. 'Darcy? Which century are you from!' she said and then, as if realising something, 'Oh, wait! You must be like 150 years old! No wonder!'

'No, I am not! I'm brand new!' I snapped.

'But...' she said.

'But what!' I was running out of patience.

'No, it's just that all the good vampires are usually around 150 years of age. Edward Cullen, the Salvatore brothers, the Originals...'

I had to laugh at that. I wasn't sure if I found her cluelessness adorable or so beyond exasperating that I was actually laughing darkly.

'Good vampires?' I said. 'Wow. Any more theories?'

'No, just a question. Do you sparkle in the sun?'

And that was it. I lost it. The nerve of this misled, puny little thing to ask me that. What was she thinking, this was some kind of joke? I let out my Scary Predator sound once again but I suppose, this time, I was just trying to reassure myself. 'You know, just for that, I am going to rip your carotid artery right now and show you what vampires are *really* like,' I said.

At which point, this relentless bimbo pulled out her phone in excitement and went, 'Oooh! Hot! But wait, before that, I want to get a picture with you! This girl in my class—Alisha—has also been waiting for her vampire soul mate forever and it would kill her if she knew I met one before her. But then, you know, she can't handle being number two at anything, so she'll probably say she wants a werewolf. By the way, do you know any werewo—'

'Enough!' I screamed. 'Are you saying there are more of *you* out there?' I really needed to know. This could mean the end of vampirism as we know it. And it would definitely mean leaving this town once and for all.

'More of me? What's that supposed to mean?' she asked.

'More airheads who think vampires are cute.'

'Awwwwwww,' she said. I swear—it's the one sound in the universe that causes me physical pain. 'Is that what this is about?'

'What is what about?'

'You feel like I'm robbing you of your manhood?' Now she was stroking my cheek and speaking in that baby voice that made me want to snap her neck just so I could end this conversation. 'Don't worry,' she added, still speaking in that voice. 'I believe you're a *beeeeeg, baaaaad* monshtah!'

I wrapped my hands tightly around my head to prevent it

from exploding. 'Just tell me how many more of you there are,' I said.

'That is confidential information!' The audacity, I tell you.

'What?' I snapped.

'Which I will be willing to share with you if you take me out on a date.' She ran her fingers down my chest in what I can only call the most embarrassing human attempt at seduction ever! What was wrong with this chick and how was I supposed to deal with it if this were some kind of epidemic? What chance does one vampire stand against a world of deluded women? And she wanted to go on a date with me? Where was she getting all this from? When did vampires go from being scary to cute? What have I missed? Questions, questions. Maybe that's it. If a date was what it took to deal with this crazy phenomenon once and for all, then so be it. I was just going to allow myself to be martyred at the altar of human idiocy for the greater good. I'm kidding. I was just going to get this over with as soon as possible and come up with a way to jolt these silly women out of their delusions.

I held my head once again and let out a groan.

'What's wrong?' she asked, her fingers still doing God knows what on my chest.

'Are you trying to seduce me?' I asked.

She winked.

'Listen to me!' I yelled. 'I am a supernatural being. I am not seducible!'

You'd think she'd break at that and begin to cry or something. Weren't girls supposed to cry easily? Well, this one just grinned and said, 'We'll see about that.'

I was beginning to get worried for myself. I wasn't sure if I had it in me to endure an entire date with this Katherine Heigl movie.

'Just tell me how many of you there are,' I said in a final attempt to cut to the chase. At this point, I was almost begging her.

'Just tell me you'd take me out for a drink!'

'Fine.'

We decided to meet at the neighbourhood bar the next evening. It was a date.

§○○ℛ

I walked in, wearing jeans and my favourite leather jacket. It was chilly and besides, I wanted to blend in. Bad idea. Because it turns out, I looked every bit like the new age vampire. You know? The broody, good-looking ones who fall in love, feed on squirrels, smile crookedly and chuckle softly? Yeah, you can imagine how much gushing I had to endure. After two hours and countless glasses of bourbon (again, bad idea—the Salvatore brothers' favourite drink, she told me), I had had enough. I turned to her to make one last point and just get the hell out of that bar. And that town, forever.

'Now that you've wasted my entire evening with your crap

theories, you listen to this,' I said and I had her attention. 'We do not sparkle in the sun, there is no such thing as a good vampire and for crying out loud, we are killers, not lovers!'

She calmly sipped her cosmopolitan through my outrage. 'Yeah, yeah, you're a big, bad monster. I get it.' Huh? 'But what *you* don't get,' she continued, this time ruffling my hair like I was a six-year-old, 'is that, this is only the pilot episode! By the time we reach the end of season 1, you'll be a changed man. And by season 2, you'd be head over heels in love with me!' I don't know if I appeared baffled or resigned, but she then lifted my chin with her index finger in smouldering seductress fashion (at least that's what I think she was trying to go for) and said, 'We have a long way to go, bad boy.'

'Okay,' I said. At least it was starting to make sense now. 'I thought you were an airhead, but you're a full-fledged delusional psych case!'

'Says the guy who rips carotid arteries for sport!'

'I'm a psycho,' I clarified. 'You're a psych *case*. Big difference.'

'Really? And what makes you so sure that someone didn't decide that for us?'

You know how they say, 'I'm not drunk enough for this conversation'? The thing is, *I was*. I was very, very drunk and yet she kept outdoing me. I was afraid to even ask what she meant. What, was she expecting some kind of Shakespearian romance here? Well, this was definitely going to end with one person dying, so I suppose we weren't too far from the fantasy. But still. Why was she not afraid of me? It just didn't make any sense. I sighed.

'Fine, I'll bite,' I said, totally not intending the pun. 'What do you mean by that?'

'How can you be sure that we're not just characters in someone's vampire romance novel or TV show? How can you know for a fact that we're not sitting here right now having our meet-cute moment?' I have to admit, she got to me. I was actually nervous now.

'No way. No fucking way. You're just drunk.'

'Am I?' she smiled, as if to challenge me.

'Yes,' I said firmly. 'You're just trying to twist this horror story into some disgusting *One Tree Hill* type teen soap. Besides, if I'm in a TV show, let it be known that it will be like *Dexter*, *Homeland* or *Breaking Bad*. NOT *Twilight*!'

'Okay, facts—*Twilight* is not a TV show and *One Tree Hill* is not disgusting.'

'Okay, there you go. No further proof necessary.'

'Proof for what?'

'So here's the thing. Even if I *could* date someone, I would never date a chick who watches *One Tree Hill*.' I thought that should put her off. If she wasn't intimidated by the fact that I was a vampire, perhaps she would be turned off by the fact that I was a snob. But *no*. This wasn't my lucky night by any stretch of imagination.

'Ah,' she said, brightening up again. 'So you admit you *could* date.'

'No, I do not. I meant that hypothetically.'

'Would you hypothetically rip my neck just to prove to me that you're the big, bad, ruthless monster you say you are?' She inched closer and closer to me. And God, you should have heard the way she said it. Like, she really believed this whole thing was a joke and that I wasn't hurting her because I actually cared about her.

I gave her a shove. 'What the hell's the matter with you?'

'So, you're not even seduced by the scent of my blood?' She was finally upset. 'You mean you've not been sitting there this whole time just fighting the urge to devour me whole?'

I couldn't believe what I witnessing. She was actually feeling rejected! I wondered what they had been feeding these women on TV. And believe it or not, I felt like I owed her an explanation. I was beginning to feel sorry for her. 'It doesn't work like that,' I said.

'Well, enlighten me.' She was trying to be stoic, but I could tell nothing could make up for the fact that I didn't want to drain her of every drop of blood in her body.

'Well,' I said. 'We are predators. We enjoy the hunt more than the kill. And *you* seem to have taken it upon yourself to strip me of my hunting urges by baby-talking me. Congratulations! My vampire erection has completely gone down.'

'Awwwwww!' That awful sound again. 'You see what's happening here?'

'No,' I said.

'You're fighting against your nature when you're around me! That's true love right there!'

'I am not fighting against my nature, I am *turned off*!' I clarified.

'Exactly! You can't kill when you're around me! That's love! You don't want to kill me!'

'Oh, I want to kill you, believe me.'

'Awwww! You're like a combination of both the Salvatore brothers.'

'Who the hell *are* the Salvatore brothers?'

'Never mind. But you know what, I'm even more convinced now that we're in a story.'

'Why's that?'

'Because,' she said, taking one last giant swig of her Cosmopolitan, 'it's the perfect new beginning. A *fresh* meet-cute. I mean the whole vampire-meets-girl-falls-irrevocably-in-love-and-fights-the-urge-to-stay-away-from-her-but-can't thing is done to death already. So if anyone is writing vampire fiction now, it has to be the girl pursuing the vampire.' I was chilled to my undead bones as I took that in. *It made sense.*

'Oh, my God,' I said. 'That almost makes sense.'

'Yep!' she said, grinning away.

'My point is, why are they even writing vampire romance? Why have they done this to us?'

'Because, fiction has to keep surprising people. Everyone's done with the Dracula variety. How can you keep vampires alive in fiction if they're going to keep popping out of the same old dusty coffins, wearing those ridiculous capes and living with bats? So we surprise them. We make them wear leather jackets, put them in high school, make them fall in love, sparkle in the sun…and boom!'

I was all out of arguments. I had completely bought in to this theory. I was just angry now. This whole night had felt like quicksand.

'That is not surprising!' I said. 'The word you're looking for is something on the lines of appalling, misleading, absurd, ludicrous!'

'Okay, okay,' she said, as if she was being the patient, enduring one in this equation. 'Like I said, you're more like the Salvatore brothers. Except, I'm the one coming after you. Which makes *you* the chosen one and me, the brooding, tormented lover.'

'Alright, that's it,' I got up to leave. 'This has been fun, but I have to go. I have people to kill and cities to terrorise.'

'See, you keep saying that, but…'

'Oh, I will totally do it. Just don't want to give you the pleasure of being my prey. I will go out there tonight and terrorise everyone in this neighbourhood till you take back your crap theories about vampires and your delusions about being in a TV show.' I couldn't believe what I had become. The kind of vampire that had to be challenged to a kill. But this wasn't over yet, of course.

'You think anyone's going to be scared of you out there?' she snorted. Snorted! 'Trust me, no girl is going to give you the pleasure of hunting her. We are all already primed to think you are the soul mate we've been destined to meet. Also, like I said, we don't even get to decide this. We just do as the writer says.' She leaned in, her face just an inch from mine. 'And *you* can run all you want, but if you're the chosen one and I'm your epic love, then I am coming after you and you are falling in love with me.' It had been years since I'd experienced fear of any kind, but I tell you, just right then, I was afraid.

'Then what happens? In the, umm, story?' I asked. You see, I'm a control freak. I'm more at ease when I know what's coming even if I can do nothing to stop it. So if I'm going to be eaten by a shark (or seduced by an airhead, same thing), I prefer to know it before it happens. That way, I can be mentally prepared.

'Then we fall in love and decide to be together,' she said, completely enjoying the role reversal. 'But in the last episode of season 1, something scary happens. It's usually a third character who is brought in to cause conflict between us. Your hot brother or my bitchy friend. Or, oh, your archenemy, the werewolf falls in love with me.'

I groaned. In part pain and part disgust. 'Yuck. This is like

One Tree Hill with supernatural creatures! I won't have it! I won't!'

'Except, it's so much more exciting than that, because in *our* story, people die!'

I sighed in relief. At least I was still a vampire, still a blood hound. 'Oh, thank God,' I said. 'So I'm still a killer.'

'Oh no, not you, love! You become the good vampire. Meaning, you only feed on squirrels and bunnies. The killers are the bad ones whom you have to protect me from.' I spoke too fast. I wanted to tell her that I didn't see it panning out that way. That if another vampire wanted to take her down, I'd gladly help. But I found myself not wanting to hurt her feelings. I mean, she was clearly into me. Crap, I was changing already. Since when did I care about human emotions?

'This is bullshit!' I said, slamming my fists on the table and standing up dramatically. 'I am not going to be in any story that turns me into some pansy-ass lover! And that's not negotiable!'

'Aww, I'm sorry, love. But that's not your decision to make! You're already *in* the story. And everything you do, like it or not, will only fulfil it.'

'Fine, then,' I said, about to leave. 'We'll see how this story ends.'

'Wait! Here's my number!' she scribbled something on a paper napkin to hand out to me.

'Oh, I'm sure fate will find a way if it's meant to be,' I said and walked away without looking back..

℘℘℘

I sat down, spent. Dr Quack kept watching me like there was more.

'That's it. I'm done.' I said.

'Okay, so what do you think?' he said.

'What do *I* think?' I'm paying you what I'm paying, to find out what *I* think?'

'Correction, I'm paying you. And no complaints, you're extremely entertaining. Have you considered writing a novel?'

'*Are you kidding me?*' By now, I was very low on patience, as you can imagine. The whole point of telling him the story and reliving the most emotionally scarring experience of my life was to get some sort of valid insight into my psyche from this genius. And yet here he was, telling me to write a novel with that smug face of his. I was left with little choice. I had to show him who I was.

I let out my Scary Predatory sound and teamed it with my Scary Predator face for a 360 degree experience. But before the fangs could come out, he had pressed some sort of panic button and before I knew it, they were injecting me with all kinds of crap and I was chained and restrained and put in this cuckoo's nest for God knows how long.

℘℘℘

It feels like a week or two. And in this time, something peculiar has taken place. It all started with me turning the TV on and tuning into a random channel where I happened to hear the word vampire. The introduction was funny enough coming from a suitably intense and broody voice:

For over a century, I have lived in secret. Hiding in the shadows, alone in the world. Until now. I am a vampire and this is my story.

I laughed my way through seasons 1 and 2. I mean, there were vampires in high school, doppelgangers, werewolves and vampires indulging in all kinds of promiscuity and oh, a vampire and werewolf hybrid. And just in case, you weren't completely sold on the supernatural world of it all, there were also witches and warlocks and dead people walking in and out of the real world. I particularly enjoyed this episode where this human cheated on his witch girlfriend with the ghost of his vampire ex girlfriend. I mean, *that's* imagination.

But I'm on season 5 now. And there's no looking back. I'm too far gone. I'm willing to give it all up, sell my soul or whatever for the answer to one burning question—will Damon and Elena ever be able to live happily ever after?

৪০৫৪

SUMMER SHOWERS

HARSH SNEHANSHU

'That is the most special thing you've ever said to me,' I said on the phone. It was a mid-July afternoon, the year was 2008 and summer was at its peak. Delhi was searing in its grip. I had, for the first time in my life, a female friend to talk to. Twenty kilometres away, she lived and studied in North Delhi, whereas I was in the South.

'I'd just said that you are the person I trust the most—how could that be counted as special? Are you so elated because you're being trusted for the first time?' she retorted.

'The sheer fact that you are telling me that means a lot to me. I can't express how happy I am!'

'See, I am so good—at flattery,' she said. Witty digs, no pretence. This was her way with words. This was what made me fond of her.

'But you're much better at being mean.'

'I know... Let me ask you something—do you trust me?' she asked.

'Of course. I trust your flattery, 100 per cent. That is the only thing that gives me a better opinion of myself.'

'Oh, poor child! You know what? You're gifted at seeking sympathy. No matter what I say, you find a way to turn my flattery into genuine appreciation. Like now, see? Nobody else could do that. I am actually a mean woman. But you, sir, are different. Perhaps that's why I like you, that's why I trust you and that's why I love you,' she said.

An awkward silence followed; for I was confused. She didn't say anything either. The ease with which she had said the last three words gave me a series of goosebumps. I could not believe that she could throw it at me just like that. We had been more of phone friends, having met just thrice. Nothing spectacular had transpired during these three meetings, though we had explored common interests and together, moved beyond being acquaintances.

෯෨ඦ

She was a friend of a friend. It was during the friend's birthday party that I had first met her. While the rest of the attendees were busy dancing to the DJ's tunes, she was standing at the balcony, looking at the stars. Being a terrible dancer, I thought it was better to go look at the stars than make a fool of myself in front of over a hundred people. She didn't acknowledge my presence for a long time, busy discerning faint stars in Delhi's polluted night sky.

'Can you spot Orion?' she had asked without even looking at me. I looked around, to ensure if what she had said was directed at me. It was. There was no one else in the balcony.

'Umm,' I said and swayed my vision across. I could locate three collinear stars—the Belt of Orion, the Hunter. 'Yes,' I pointed out, 'there it is—see the belt above that bunch of stars.'

'Were you ogling below Orion's belt? Shame shame, very bad. The poor fellow is not even dressed,' she said. I grinned.

'Okay, try finding Big Dipper,' she had asked. This one was easier. I indicated it instantly.

'Locate the Pole star,' I asked.

She smirked, as if I'd asked a trivial question, and directed towards it. 'Have you ever noticed how all these constellations are named?'

'No.' I hadn't, but I wanted to know. 'How?'

'There are subliminal meanings behind them. Note the names—Big, Pole, Orion's Belt, don't you see?'

'Really?' I asked.

'Yes.'

'Strange. All these astronomers, it looks to me, are perverts.' I was being self-righteous, playing on my prudish self to cast a good impression. But she didn't seem impressed.

'So are we. What's wrong in being a pervert? Perversion is just a bad word for curiosity.'

'Hmm.'

'See, I'll show you. Look at that bunch of stars, the ones which form a circle. Don't they look like a nipple?'

'What?' I was not sure whether she had said what I heard.

'Nipple. What's so scandalous about it?'

'No, nothing. Yes, they do,' I said, trying to fit myself into the situation. How could someone be so comfortable with a stranger? She seemed different from most girls I'd met before. There was no air of superiority around her.

'Look at you. Your face is flushed red. It's okay. It's just a nipple I'm talking about. I wonder what you would have done if I had shown you a constellation that looks like a phallus?' She'd followed her statement with an endearing wink—a wink that signified a rapport, despite us not having exchanged our names with each other.

With her directness, she had made me question conventional definitions of right and wrong, and good and bad that I had been spoon-fed since childhood. Coming from a small-town, I didn't know that things that the society tries to conceal could be seen and talked about with such openness, without judgment. My prudishness and formality took some time, but eventually vanished in her candid company.

'Is there really one?' I asked.

'Yes, sir. But don't worry, I'm not going to make you feel more uncomfortable.'

'No, no. Show me.'

'Haha. Haven't you seen it enough times to be bored of it already?' she asked. I broke into cheeky laughter. After much persuasion, she showed me the phallic constellation, along with constellations that had even weirder shapes. There was a distorted snout, and to beat them all, a gigantic bum. She shared how the habit of sky gazing was inculcated in her by her grandfather, who used to have a small telescope which he passed on to her. Every time she would visit him at the family house in the small town of Charkhi Dadri, a hundred kilometres away from Delhi, she would watch the clear night sky from the roof of her ancestral house.

'There is no pollution there in the countryside—you can almost see the Milky Way, a faint cloudy stretch of white in the sky,' she had said.

'O! O! Milky, the word. Did you notice the subliminal meaning hidden there?'

'Well, somebody is fast,' she said, and added, 'and perverted,' with a wink.

In those fifty minutes of sky gazing, I had gotten so enchanted with her that I wanted to meet her again. It was only while leaving that we'd exchanged our names. On the pretext of inviting her to my upcoming college festival, I asked for her number. She passed it on without hesitating, without any fuss.

A week later, I invited her to the college festival, which turned out to be rather interesting. There was a salsa workshop where my terrible dancing was complemented by her exquisite moves, hand in hand, leg in leg, moving from the zone of awkwardness to a realm of comfort. I was surprised to find that unlike what I had thought, she was actually a brilliant dancer. It was the loud music that she despised, that had brought her out to the balcony last time.

On our third meet, she had wanted to catch up with me because she happened to be in South Delhi. We had a decent conversation over coffee about books and authors. Both of us loved reading. While she liked classics, authors like Jane Austen, Mark Twain, Oscar Wilde—the man behind her nimble wit; I was more into contemporary fiction, fond of Jhumpa Lahiri, Khalid Hosseini and Julian Barnes—all of them serious fiction writers, with little room for wit. Little did I know that the conversation that began with constellations would continue for over three months, moving on to books, authors, dance, music, puzzles, family, aspirations and emotions.

৪০০৪

'What? What did you say just now? Did you mean it or was it just flattery?' I asked. Amidst fear and anticipation, I both wanted and didn't want the answer.

'What? I meant whatever I said.'

'You mean...you mean you love me?'

'Yes! I love you...as a very good friend of mine.'

'I joked earlier that you are mean, but now I mean it. You are the meanest person I know,' I said, irritated.

'What is this, silly? You get angry when things don't go according to your wishes. I told you that I love you, isn't that enough? Why are you bombarding me with yet another bag full of your tantrums—seeking needless sympathy?'

'Don't change the topic,' I said.

'You should know that you sound adorable when you're irritated,' she said.

'Stop kidding! This is serious. Now that things have gone down this track, let me tell you something. I like you. I like you in a different way than how I would like a friend.'

'Like a brother likes his sister?'

'Shut up. I'm serious, for God's sake. Don't give me a reason to hate you now.'

'Sorry, go on. I am not used to appreciation. Being liked makes me feel like a Facebook post, you see.'

'You are impossible,' I sighed.

'Get to the point. You were saying that you like me in a way different than how you would like a friend. Elaborate,' she demanded. It felt good to know that she bothered to remember what I was saying, because I'd forgotten what I'd said by now.

'What if I told you that I love you? In a way that makes me want to be there with you all the time—in times when you need somebody by your side, and in times when you're bored.'

'You contradicted your own statement, silly. I won't need

you when I am bored because I am sure you'll be the one responsible for it.'

'Everything is a joke to you, isn't it? Can't you see how much courage I had to muster to say what I'd said? I have never said that to anybody else. Let alone say it, I have never ever felt this way about anyone else before. I want to be more than just a friend to you. Will you let me?'

'Yes, as a friend and a driver. I needed one anyway. Drop me off to college every morning, pick me up thereafter and drop me back to my hostel. It will make me feel safe as well as save my money. How much money are you willing to work for? Would twenty rupees a day suffice?'

'I am going to hang up now.'

'I know you will not hang up. If you will, then how will you know my answer?'

'What do you want?' I asked, exasperated.

'I want to leave it to God.' At this point, I knew she had lost it.

'Wow, what a sick choice! Leaving it to God. Why are you talking to me then? Go and talk to your damned God!'

'Okay, bye. Will I find him in the Yellow Pages?'

I kept quiet, trying hard not to laugh. There was nothing I could say to her without being made a joke out of.

'Wait for tomorrow. If it rains, I shall say *yes*,' she said, breaking the silence.

'What the hell is that? It's late July and haven't you seen

the sun? There is no probability that it will rain. You are being unfair to me.'

'If God has a positive answer for me, then it will rain.'

I was not sure whether God had a positive answer for her or not, but I was entirely sure that whatever be the case, God would definitely have a negative answer for me. It had always been like that. Nothing good had ever happened to me just by chance; in fact bad things happened to me when I was least responsible for them. As a child, while my friends made noise, teachers considered me the culprit and caned me. Friends cheating from my answer-sheet during exams got better grades than I did. In sports, when I practised sprinting for a year and was sure that I could defeat every other runner in the school, these three new kids from some Sainik School enrolled in my class and outran me during sports day. In college, when I wanted to become the house secretary, my roommate accidentally (or intentionally?) locked me while I was sleeping inside my room, and went home. By the time I'd managed to get the lock broken, I was too late to nominate myself for the post. God, for me, has been like the Devil, whose only role in life was to kick my ass on a daily basis. Now that I had come this close to matters of the heart, I didn't want God's propensity to goof up my life.

'You're beyond impossible,' I said and hung up on her. As I'd expected, she didn't call me back. Neither did I. We both waited silently for the next day. In spite of my scepticism, I kept looking at the sky every now and then.

The many stars twinkling across the clear skies only made me sad. The reminiscence of our first meeting, of discovering constellations and funny shapes seemed to belong to a distant past. The phallic constellation now seemed like God's way of showing me the finger.

I dragged my bed nearer to the window and stared at the sky till late in the night. Lost in thought, I didn't realise when I fell asleep. I dreamt of being weary and old, unsure and bothered, excited and hopeful, all at the same time. The next day seemed to take more than the usual time to come.

ಐದ

Drops of water slapped my eyelids hard. 'Go away,' I said, assuming it was my roommate trying to wake me up for class. It wasn't him. As I squinted at the window, I realised that the morning sun had forgotten to rise. There were clouds dancing in the rain in front of my eyes. I rubbed my eyes, unable to believe.

I picked up my phone and dialled her number right away. She was sleeping, unaware of the summer rain.

'Hey, your God answered and answered for me too! You owe me a *yes*,' I charged. It took her some time to respond. It's only after she opened her windows that she spoke.

'Your *yes* is still with me and I am too selfish to give it to you,' she said; her voice drunk with sleep.

'But why?'

'God can't be so direct. It is by chance that it rained; my belief has not been affirmed yet. If it rains again tomorrow, then I'll say yes. I promise.'

'You do know that you don't need to prove your meanness over and over again.'

'Practice makes a woman *more* perfect,' she said. She must have winked after her statement. I could almost see it through the phone.

'You know what, you think you are funny, but in fact you are lame. You are one confused and superstitious girl. Let me tell you loud and clear that I hate you,' I said and disconnected the call.

I was feeling guilty for being very rude to her right in the morning. A minute later, however, an SMS from her that washed away my guilt. It said, 'Smile. That's the second best thing you can do with your lips. And stop fantasising about the first thing, silly.'

I did smile and messaged her back a smiley simultaneously. We shared no words during the day. That night, she called.

I hung up saying, 'Let us talk tomorrow, if anything happens.'

'Not anything, silly. *Something*,' she managed to squeeze in before I cut the call.

৪৩

The second night was equally long; the daytime clouds were nowhere to be seen. The stars seemed farther away—faint and sleepy, much like I was. I strolled across the college campus all alone, thinking about the turn our relationship had taken, delving into the circumstances that led to the admission of our fondness for each other. She had said that she loved me, out of the blue, but I had confided it to her very formally, after a lot of thinking and apprehension. *Would she mind if I told her that I loved her? Would it complicate my friendship with her? Was I good enough for her?* I had gotten used to this perpetual state of hanging in between, of being stuck in a limbo, having no clear answer. Having no answer is always better than a clear negative answer. At least, hope remains. Dry winds raced through the empty roads of my college. There was no way it was going to rain the next morning.

I returned to my room and slept at the regular time. I had already done enough thinking to tire myself out. This time when I didn't long for the next morning, to remain content with whatever little hope remained in me, it arrived quite early.

॰ॐ॰

By the time I woke up, the sun had already warmed up my room. My pillow was wet with sweat. Was it anxiety or just the heat? I presumed it was the latter, since the bed was still by the window, sunlight creeping in like an unwanted guest. The rays that rudely invaded my eyes, seemed to say, 'The clouds have cleared. Now your life shall be darkened with light.'

It was rare to have classes on a Saturday, but summer courses made it worse. I had flunked in two courses the previous semester and it was the remedial summer courses that prevented me from running home, a thousand kilometres away, in Bihar. Two lectures, followed by meetings with three professors concerning summer projects didn't allow me to notice how the morning comfortably merged with dusk, bringing an end to what could have been the day of my acceptance. A tinge of orange and yellow in the far off sky became dark before one could even give them a proper look. The sudden darkness reeked of sarcasm. God had failed me, once again. It all seemed rather funny. 'Is it the end? If yes, *you are a big bore*,' I cursed God, 'at least you could have ended it on a better note, despite the same end.'

Free from work, a bit anxious to ask her to reconsider the last morning rain as God's answer, I looked at my phone intently. It showed nothing but a blank screen—much like my mind. She hadn't sent a message. Was it because she wasn't sure about me? If that was the case, I would rather ask her not to put herself through the torture of considering my inept proposal. Was it because she was as apprehensive as I was that it wouldn't rain? Did she have a plan B? What would she do if God's answer is actually no—that there is no rain? Would she refute him for me? I doubted she would.

If she had to refute God's wishes, she wouldn't have roped him in, in the first place. My train of thought was broken by an intermittent tickle in my hand. It was her on phone.

'Yes, yes, yes, yes, yes! A million times *yes*,' she cried. I'd never heard her as excited before.

'Did it rain today?' I asked. I felt numb. I had no idea what had changed her mind. *What was going on?*

'Yes, yes, yes; it is raining cats, dogs, elephants and hippos, here since the last two minutes,' she said, ecstatic. The twenty kilometre difference had made all the difference.

Was I ecstatic? Umm, *no*. I looked up at the dark night sky. A huge rain-drop struck against my spectacles with a great force and scattered all across. I didn't bother to wipe it. Soon followed more drops, some of which welled up in my eyes, but the sky had enough water to wash away my tears. It had rained. The clouds were just two minutes late.

'Some hippos have come here too,' I said, still struggling to pull myself together.

'They have found their lost brother in you.'

'Come on, my face is not like theirs. It's more like yours,' I said.

'Yeah, so should I say that I have found my lost brother in you?'

'You always make me lose when I am winning.'

'You never are,' she said.

She had won. Not only the conversation, but the game of faith as well. But there was something within me that didn't seem convinced. I was not feeling the same way I thought I would feel. How could God grant my wishes? It had never worked that way with me, had it? What if it had rained just by chance, yet again? What if we were actually unsure of each other and the rain was actually jinxing it? Three in-person meetings, a little over hundred telephone conversations, how could these little things be enough to say a yes to sharing our lives with each other? I needed more certainty.

'Listen to me. I have to tell you something,' I said.

'Now what? My stomach is already full—with joy.'

'Give me a break. Now, it's not a yes from me,' I said. This time, it didn't take me courage to say that. I was sure that this was what it was.

'Oh my God, yet another tantrum! Listen silly, don't you dare act smart. Leave that bit to me. Moreover, it doesn't suit you at all.'

'I am serious. If it rains tomorrow, then I shall say a yes. I need to convince myself that it really works.' I don't know what made me say that but I stuck to it, I meant it.

'We'll talk tomorrow then. Tomorrow never lies,' she said, a bit seriously though, still I could say for sure a wink would have followed her statement. She loved being the one-eyed queen. Cute, she was. And I was in love with her. As she was with me. All that separated the two of us was a few drops of water to fall from the sky the following day.

৪০০৫

The next day dawned, this time neither suddenly nor slowly, but at its natural but boring pace. Yet there was something new to this day. Thanks to the two days of unexpected rain, the weather had taken a pleasant turn and this called for a meeting.

'Hey, it is a Sunday.' Even after a million yes*es* from her the last evening, it was quite strange that I still employed a formal reason to propose a meeting.

'Thanks for making me realise that today you're going to stink,' she said, mocking my habit of not taking bath on weekends.

'I want to meet you and I have already taken a bath.'

'Aww, that's a surprise.'

'What? My wanting to meet you or taking a bath?'

'First tell me whether this "taking a bath" means bathing in perfumes or a proper bath,' she asked.

'Oh, so the "I want to meet you" thing is not a surprise for you.'

'Of course not. It's our day, after all.'

'How can you be so sure?' I asked, struck by her optimism.

'In the same way you always remain unsure, silly.'

I had already had a proper bath and I bathed in perfumes too. Having two baths a day does make one feel confident. Her optimism was contagious. It took me a while to choose what to wear; after all, she said that it was our day. Unable to choose, I finally decided on the blue jeans and white shirt, the same combination that I had worn the day she had come to my college for the festival. She had even complimented (I think) me about it, saying that I looked less silly than usual. I thought of buying her flowers, but couldn't decide which ones to buy—yellow ones were for friends, while red is for lovers, apparently. Unable to decide between the two colours, I bought a bunch of orange marigolds instead.

I set off. It was during those days when the metro ran only in the northern and central part of Delhi. South Delhi to Central Secretariat was either a painful bus ride, or a costly auto ride. Careful not to ruffle the creases of my ironed white shirt, I chose the costlier option—something that I would have never chosen before. I looked out at the sky, which was painfully blue, with no hint of an impending rain. But something changed within me. There was a sudden sureness about her as my auto inched towards the Central Secretariat metro station, from where I had to head to Vishwavidyalaya, where her hostel was. It took me one hour twenty minutes to reach her place—a five-storeyed hostel. She lived on the third floor, her window facing the road. I knew this because she had once described on the phone the view from her window. She had talked about the big mall road, filled with vehicles of all kinds, the rickshaws near the corner, the flurry of people near the metro station entry after the red light, the numerous hawkers who sold burgers, cold coffee and her favourite momos stall.

I looked up at the window, trying to figure if she was sitting by it, waiting for me. I knew it was too much to ask for, but still a part of me wanted to know whether she was as excited about meeting me as I was about meeting her. The bright sunlight made it impossible for me to discern anything. I called her. She didn't answer the phone though. But her SMS came within a minute of my call. It said, 'Silly, you look sillier when you look for me with your monkey*ish* face trying to fight the sunlight.'

I smiled. I looked up again, trying to make my face look less like a monkey's. She was standing there by her window, an ear to ear smile on her face. Her face disappeared abruptly and a hand holding a jug came out of the window instead. Puzzled, I stood there until the jug emptied half a litre of water over my *monkeyish* face.

Another SMS arrived, 'Silly, here is your rain. Are you convinced now that it really works?'

I replied with a smile, 'Yes, yes, yes, yes, *yes*! A million times.'

She smiled back upon reading my message. She asked for five minutes which I happily gave her. I went to the other side of the road, standing there to wait for her.

When she came out, our eyes were locked into each other's. Before I could say anything, she jumped on me giving me the tightest hug ever. A tight hug in the middle of the road, it would have certainly made me feel awkward earlier, but not that day. I gingerly returned her hug.

'I love you.'

'I love you two, three, four, five, six…' she squeaked merrily.

'I love you a zillion times,' I said, sure that I'd trumped her, at last.

'I win!' she said and winked in the same way as I always used to imagine her while speaking with her on the phone.

I was lost in her, until something kissed my cheek. It was a wet kiss. That of the rain that had just arrived.

හ෪෩

THE X-BOSS

SHOMA NARAYANAN

It all started on a Monday. I got to work late because I'd managed to lock myself out of my bathroom (it has a sliding door with a nifty little catch that clicks into place if the door is slammed too hard), and it took the building watchman half an hour to get it open. My bladder almost burst while waiting and I had to tip the watchman a hundred bucks for his efforts. Also, the door was ruined, and would need to be fixed before my landlady came around on her monthly snooping exercise.

So I was already in a bad mood when I got to work, and finding a set of rude e-mails in my inbox about a delayed pricing proposal didn't help at all. The proposal had been ready for around two weeks, but Deven, my boss, hadn't got around to signing it. I lay in wait for him, and pounced as soon as he got out of a meeting.

Me: Have you seen the pricing proposal I gave you?

Boss: What proposal?

Me: I gave it to you last week—it's a bit urgent.

Boss: (looking around vaguely) I don't think you gave it to me, Sanjana.

Me: (digging among the papers in his in-tray and handing it to him)

Boss: Humph. What happened to the market scoping exercise you were to do in Nasik?

Me: I'll get it done by month-end (We will launch in Nasik the day Rolex starts selling watches in Dharavi. He always brought up something like this when he was wrong-footed.)

Boss: (looking at me as if wondering why I was still there and not rushing off to Nasik immediately to begin scoping) Well?

Me: The proposal?

Boss: Ah that. I'll look at it.

Me: Sales is putting a lot of pressure on me.

Boss: So?

Me: Could you sign it now please?

Boss: No, I need to go through it first. You should have given it to me earlier.

I walked away, fuming. Deven was the most irritating boss I'd ever worked with. Not only was he stupid and stuck-up (a deadly combination), he also behaved as if he was doing his team a personal favour by doing any work. Pretty much everyone in his team left within a year, and I'd completed ten months and was raring to be off.

For a while, I sat around, brooding darkly. I had slogged really hard all through the year and during my mid-term appraisal my boss told me that while my work was 'at par with peer group', he felt that I needed to improve my interpersonal skills—read don't make faces at him behind his back, something he caught me doing a couple of times during meetings. Which meant he'd probably give me a mediocre rating and ruin my chances for a promotion that year.

At around twelve o' clock, Deven suddenly landed up at my desk and announced that he'd decided to take me along for the sales convention in Singapore later that week. For a minute or two, I was actually pleased, until I realised he wanted me around to take the flak for the pricing change being delayed.

'I don't know if I can get my visa done in time,' I said grumpily.

'It'll be a good networking opportunity,' he said in reproving tones. 'I expect you to have things sorted out by evening.' I spent the rest of the day running around trying to get my Singapore visa done, and quarrelling with the Thomas Cook lady who booked me onto Air India instead of Singapore Airlines. My visa got done a day before we were scheduled to leave. Other than making multiple enemies in Thomas Cook, my attempts to change to another airline didn't meet with any success. So when the Air India flight developed a technical problem, and was stranded on the tarmac for eight hours, I was stranded as well. Deven was supposed to be on the same flight, but thankfully he managed to switch to Singapore Airlines. I don't think I'd have been able to bear his conversation at one in the morning without committing homicide.

౭ఌ

I finally reached Singapore the next afternoon. There was a formal dinner organised at the hotel, but I was too pooped to go. The next day, we had a 'team building' exercise that involved an extremely juvenile sounding 'treasure hunt' across Sentosa. I liked the cable car ride to Sentosa, because I was in the same car as the sales head and could tell him that he didn't get his pricing change in time because of Dickhead Deven, and not because of anything I did. The treasure hunt, on the other hand, was terrible. We were painfully conspicuous because we had been given matching bright-red convention T-shirts to wear (mine reached to my knees because they only had men's sizes) and everyone was rushing after clues from one place to another like a herd of buffaloes in heat. As soon as I could, I dropped behind and bought myself a souvenir T-shirt in the correct size, which I changed into in the loo. Then I took a cheerful-looking orange bus to the beach.

On the beach, I ran into Josh Williams, an American who'd been deputed from our New York office to Mumbai some time back when I was a trainee. He worked in Singapore now, and he was married to South African girl he'd met in Dubai. He even had a ten-month old son called Jason.

Josh decided to come back with me to meet some of the other people he knew from the India office, Deven among them. Deven was in the midst of a heated discussion with our Amit Khanna, who was our Sales Head, and cordially detested Deven. They broke off when they saw Josh. Deven was a compulsive ass-licker, and though Josh was technically junior to him, his being a *firang* from the regional office automatically elevated his ass to a lickable level.

Josh's wife dropped by to pick him up along with their son and Deven convinced her to join us for dinner at the hotel restaurant. Monique was a tall, well-built red-head, and Jason was a scarily well-behaved baby. He sat quietly in his stroller and played with his toes instead of bawling his head off like every other kid I've ever been to a restaurant with. Either he was on sedatives, or *firang* kids are naturally better behaved than Indian ones.

We were halfway through dinner, when Deven complained of a pain in the chest. Josh asked. 'Is it bad, Deven? Should we get hold of a doctor?'

'Attention-seeking fusspot,' I thought to myself, but then Deven stood up. His face looked really odd, like he was trying to say something, and couldn't get the words out. And then he collapsed without a sound. Monique gave a little frightened scream, and Josh rushed to his side. A few waiters came over, and they helped get Deven out of the restaurant. Monique and I followed them. The hotel doctor was called, and he said that it looked like a massive heart attack. Deven didn't seem to be breathing.

The next ten minutes rushed by. An ambulance was called, and Deven was taken to the nearest hospital. Josh and Amit Khanna followed in Josh's car, and I was left sitting in the lobby with Monique. Her face was a picture of concern 'Poor man!' she exclaimed. 'He seemed like such a nice person. And he's quite young isn't he?'

I agreed that Deven was quite young (he must have been around thirty-five), and carefully refrained from making any comments about his niceness.

ಸಂಞ

Amit Khanna called on my cell phone. 'Sanjana, Deven didn't make it,' he said.

I had been expecting the news—Deven had looked as dead as it was possible for a man without a visible mark on him to look—but I was still a little shaken up. Poor man, he might have been a jerk, but he certainly didn't deserve this.

'Do you need me to come down there, Amit?' I asked.

'No, we've got it covered,' he said. 'Josh is helping out with the paperwork, and Sushil from HR will be taking the body back to India. Deven's brother is making arrangements for the funeral.'

ಸಂಞ

The next day was a blur. The conference continued, though the 'gala dinner' was cancelled. I made Deven's presentation to the top team—I had worked on the slides, so it wasn't tough, but I felt terrible, as if I was taking advantage of his death to try and step into his shoes.

I was back in India the next day and in office the day after. The rest of our team was not part of the conference, and they clustered around me ghoulishly to get details of what happened. They were shocked, but no one was noticeably upset—Deven had trodden on all our toes way too often.

The business head, Saket Nagpal, called me and Amit into his cabin later that day. The economic downturn was just beginning to make its presence felt, and there were rumours of a recruitment freeze. After the initial shock of Deven's death, they were both concentrating on how to re-structure Deven's department so as to benefit Amit the most.

The structure they'd come up with had me reporting to Amit while taking on most of what Deven used to handle. It was a much larger role for me, and my promotion looked like it was within reach again. With one senior resource less reflecting on his head-count chart, Saket could afford to be generous.

When I got back to my flat that evening, there was a little parcel waiting for me. It was done up in a lot of brown tape, and I carried it into the kitchen looking for something to open it with. I was thirsty, and I poured myself a Coke from a half-empty bottle that had been lying in the fridge for a week. It had gone flat, and looked like dishwater. I sipped at it while I hacked through the layers of tape—it tasted a bit like dishwater too—and I narrowly missed slicing an inch off my index finger.

The parcel was a set of books I had ordered from an online bookstore. Deven had caught me checking out the website when I was supposed to have been working on the next quarter's budgets. For once, he hadn't read me a lecture, but he did ask me to order a book for him that he hadn't been able to get in Mumbai. I pulled it out—it was a book of plays by Noel Coward. It wasn't really my kind of book, but I started reading 'Blithe Spirit' to see what it was like. The humour was a little forced, but the plot was good—it was about a middle-aged playwright whose dead first wife materialises during a séance he organises to gather material for a new play.

'The other two plays aren't as good,' said a familiar snooty voice, and I turned to see Deven sitting on the edge of my sofa. Maybe because I'd been reading a play about ghosts, or maybe because I was very sleepy, I didn't scream or faint or do anything silly. I just looked straight at Deven, and said, 'You're not supposed to be here.'

He grunted and said, 'I agree. I was about to leave, when I saw you reading my book.'

'You can have it back,' I said. 'Why are you here, anyway? You're dead.'

He looked annoyed, the way he used to when I interrupted him during one of his interminable monologues.

'You called me back. You should know.'

I gasped in shock. '*I called you back?* Why would I do that?' Then I realised that I sounded really rude (even if this was a dream, which I was 99 per cent sure it was). 'I mean, I'm sorry you're dead, and all that, but I definitely didn't do anything to bring you back. Unless I did it involuntarily like the parlour maid in the play.'

He grunted again.

'Look, Deven,' I said uncomfortably, 'I'm really sorry, but you can't stay here.'

'I wouldn't dream of staying.' He gave my messy living-room a disdainful look. 'I'll need some help with transport though.'

I stared at him. 'I don't have a car. Sorry, but you'll have to find your own way.'

He muttered to himself, then hauled himself off my sofa and marched to the door, a picture of outraged dignity.

'Good night, Deven,' I said chirpily and showed him out.

୫୦୯୨

Next morning, I remembered about the dream only when I was in a cab on my way to office, and I felt rather guilty about the way I'd treated him. The feeling of guilt persisted, until I reached my desk, and found him sitting in my chair. This time, I did scream. A couple of guys rushed over from the next cubicle.

'Sanjana, is everything okay?' asked one of them.

I pointed to my chair. He looked at it, and back at me, puzzled. Evidently he couldn't see Deven, otherwise he'd be screaming louder than me.

'A cockroach,' I said weakly. 'It's gone now.'

He made a face and said, 'I'll tell Housekeeping. Don't worry; it's probably far away now.'

I waited till he went back to his desk, and glared at Deven.

'What the hell are *you* doing here?'

'This is *my* desk!'

'Uhh, actually, it's *mine* now.'

'They gave you my *job*?'

'Well, you couldn't expect them to leave it vacant, could you? Now will you please get out of my chair?'

He got up and walked huffily across to the filing cabinet. 'I spent thirteen years in this company. And the day I die, they hand my flat over to someone else, and give my job to *you*, of all people. I suppose they've given my car away as well.'

'That's what death does to you,' I said. 'Now be a good ghost, and go away and haunt someone else. Amit Khanna, maybe? He's the one who's actually got your job. I only get to do the work.'

Deven flatly refused to go haunt anyone else. There was, of course, the basic disadvantage that no one could see him other than me. Not much point haunting people who walked through him, or, like Amit Khanna, almost sat on him. So he hung around my cubicle, and pretty soon I was at the end of my tether.

හ❍ශ

Four days after he'd materialised, I walked into office to see Deven sitting at my desk with his head in his hands. I began to feel a little sorry for him, and reached out to pat him on his shoulder. He jumped back, and I felt a warm breeze waft over my fingers, as they passed through his arm. Funny, I'd thought ghosts were supposed to be cold.

'Don't touch me,' he said. 'I hate having people's hands go through me.'

'I'm sorry,' I said, sounding apologetic though his being permeable was definitely not my fault. Besides, he wasn't even listening to me.

'This is driving me crazy,' he said. 'I need to get away from here.'

'If you haven't noticed, Deven, I'm not exactly holding you back,' I said.

'You are definitely the most insensitive woman I've ever met,' he said angrily. 'You know I can't get around without you.'

After he'd talked for a bit, I figured he wanted me to take a week off and take him to visit his brother in Bengaluru.

'I'm saving my leave for my wedding,' I said.

'Oh yes, how could I forget? You're marrying that long-haired graphic designer chap.' (He'd met Varun once at an office party, and they hadn't got along, to put it mildly.) 'Bad choice, if you ask me. Does he know you've started seeing ghosts?'

He had a point there. I hadn't had the guts to tell anyone about him. Especially not Varun, who was a staunch rationalist. If I'd told him that I was communing with the shade of my ex-boss, he'd have sent out for a strait-jacket. Telling Amit Khanna or Saket would have been a seriously career-limiting move. I finally decided to tell Josh, who was the 'there are more things in heaven and earth' sorts—he'd even been through a major spiritualism phase when he was in India.

I popped into Amit's cabin, and used his phone to call Josh. I could see Deven mooning around my cubicle. Poor bugger, he could touch things, but he couldn't move them—a paperclip on my desk could be Mount Fujiyama for all the luck he was having picking it up. Finally he gave up, and started staring moodily at my computer screen.

Josh picked up on the fourth ring. Bringing up the topic was incredibly awkward and finally I blurted it all out, true dumb-chick-in-horror-movie style.

'You're having me on,' Josh said when I finally stopped talking.

'I swear I'm not.'

'Then you're imagining it. Your subconscious is taking this way out to get away from the shock of Deven's death.' Damn, I'd forgotten about Josh's Freudian phase.

'Josh, if it was my sub-conscious, I'd have dreamt up someone like Heath Ledger, not Deven Bhat! Granted, his dying like that was shock, but I swear I wasn't traumatised enough to start seeing ghosts.'

Josh was no use. All he could suggest was getting Deven to Singapore and leaving him behind somehow. Because he'd died there. It was the lamest idea ever—I should have asked my mum, she'd at least have recommended a reliable tantric.

श৹঩

As it turned out, I did end up taking Deven to Singapore. It happened this way—Varun suddenly decided that we'd been seeing each other for long enough, and he needed to make an honest woman of me immediately. He insisted on having a simple registered wedding, because his atheist principles did not allow him to participate in a religious ceremony. I wasn't too keen on a big circus of a wedding with my mum playing ringmaster, so I agreed.

We got married in a little registry office lined with green Godrej almirahs. We had planned to go to Greece for our honeymoon, but Varun's visa got rejected. The only valid visa that both of us had was for Singapore, and tickets were surprisingly cheap.

We were due to leave the morning after the wedding. Both sets of parents came over for dinner, finally leaving at around ten o' clock at night. My mother cornered me in the kitchen to give me some hurried 'first night' advice.

Poor mum, she was trying really hard to pretend she was fine with her long-haired son-in-law and the wedding among the almirahs. I suddenly felt very sorry for her, and I listened to her patiently without telling her that she was a couple of years too late with the advice.

I think it was the whole 'first night' conversation that put me off the thought of sex—my mum had made it sound like the first, slightly unpleasant task in a long list of post-wedding to-dos. We lay in bed, talking softly for a long while, and then drifted off to sleep.

৵৹ৎ

I woke up at around five o' clock and wandered into the kitchen for a drink of water. I was still half-asleep, and I nearly jumped out of my skin when I heard Deven's voice say reproachfully, 'You didn't even tell me the date of your wedding.'

'Holy shit!' I said furiously. 'What are you doing here—*it's my wedding night!*'

Apparently, he'd walked the whole way, when I didn't turn up for work. Even for a spook, this was seriously spooky behaviour.

Varun was still asleep. I called Josh. It was later in the day in Singapore, and he was awake and getting ready for work.

'Right, I'll do it.'

'Do what?'

'Bring Deven across.'

Now that I'd agreed, Josh wasn't so keen on the idea, and he kept throwing out feeble excuses that I mowed down firmly. I had had enough of handling Deven. Josh could take over, whether he could see him or not.

§℧℧

It was difficult getting Deven into the flight, because he was still not used to people walking through him, and he gave out startled yelps whenever he walked into someone's hand baggage. Of course, I couldn't tell Varun, even though Deven was sitting next to him all through the flight (thankfully there was a seat vacant). Both Deven and I winced whenever Varun put a hand or elbow through him—Deven was convinced that I was making him do it on purpose, and kept up a stream of waspish conversation that drove me bananas.

Josh met us 'by accident' in the lobby of the hotel as we were checking in. And—break-through! Josh could see him too. I could tell by the way his eyes widened and followed Deven around as he dodged behind Varun to escape having a huge trolley full of luggage go through him.

I told Varun that I'd join him in a couple of minutes and stayed behind to talk to Josh.

'Man, all this while I was sure you were off your rocker. I can't believe this. Can he hear us?'

'Yes, I can,' said Deven huffily. 'Glad to see you, Josh— I thought I'd go crazy hanging out with these two love-birds.'

I scowled at him, but didn't protest. Some of Varun's conversation in the flight had been embarrassingly explicit—of course he didn't know that my ex-boss was sitting next to him, lapping up every word. Josh offered to take Deven home with him, and I thankfully agreed.

I couldn't say that my honeymoon was a success. I was too stressed out, expecting Deven to reappear at any moment. Varun noticed it, but didn't comment, probably attributing my edginess to post-wedding jitters.

Josh was having a rough time too. I sneaked downstairs and called him from the lobby at least once every day. Deven had lodged himself firmly into their family. Monique could see him, and so could Jason probably, because Josh thought he saw him watching Deven once. However, as Jason commonly ignored all adults not equipped with either breasts or milk bottles, they weren't sure. Josh's theory was that everyone who was with Deven when he died could see him. What worried him was Monique—she seemed to be inordinately pleased with their house guest.

'You mean she likes having him around?' I asked in amazement.

'She's always been into supernatural stuff. But it's not just that.' Josh looked really harassed. 'She's been getting really bored at home with just Jason for company. Somehow, she hasn't made too many friends around here. And she and Deven have a lot in common. They spend the whole day discussing books and music and movies. I've been trying to hint to her that we should be figuring out some way of getting him back onto his astral plane or wherever he should be, but she only gets annoyed.' I couldn't quite fathom it. Monique had seemed sensible enough when I'd met her—why would she want to hang out with an idiot (albeit a dead one) like Deven?

The situation got more and more complicated, because Varun caught me having coffee with Josh when I'd told him I was going shopping, and he was uncharacteristically upset. By our fifth day in Singapore, we were barely talking to each other. Josh finally decided to smooth things over by inviting us to dinner at a seafood restaurant near the Singapore Flier.

The Flier is a huge Ferris wheel, like the London Eye. Varun and I went for a spin in it before dinner. We were a little late getting to the restaurant because I wasted some time and heaps of money in the souvenir shop. Josh had booked us a table in an alcove secluded from the rest of the restaurant.

Varun's mood had improved, and he greeted Josh happily. My spirits, on the other hand, plummeted when I realised that Deven was part of the dinner party. Monique got up and hugged me enthusiastically. I hugged her back, and raised an eyebrow at Deven over her shoulder.

'I do need to get out once in a while,' he said huffily.

'Of course you do,' began Monique, and then suddenly clammed up when she encountered furious glares from both me and Josh.

Varun hadn't noticed, luckily. He sat down, and began scrutinising a menu.

'Maybe you should order for all of us,' he said to Josh. 'I don't even know what half these things are.'

'Oh, I'm as bad as you are,' said Josh, as he beckoned to a waiter. 'I jab at the menu and trust my luck.'

Josh and I were both distracted, going through the menu with the maitre d', otherwise we might have averted what happened next. A young waiter was going around the table shaking out the table napkins from the elaborate shapes they were folded into. He moved from Varun to Josh to Monique…and then to Deven—and he shook Deven's napkin out and tried to put it on his lap. The napkin gracefully fluttered through Deven, and landed on the chair—we could still see its outline through Deven as he tried to wriggle away from it.

The waiter's eyes were as large as saucers, and he looked like he was about to scream. Varun was still reading the menu, and hadn't noticed anything wrong. Josh and I stared at each other dumbly—we had no idea what to do. Monique gave us an exasperated look, and swiftly knocked my handbag off the table where I'd put it. It hit the floor and opened, spilling its contents (which included a sanitary towel and a box of condoms that Varun had bought in the morning) to the floor.

'Oh, I'm so sorry,' she said, and to the waiter, 'Can you help me with this, please?'

He knelt automatically, and began to pick up things, his eyes still fixed on Deven. I got up as well, and grabbed the

ST and the condoms and shoved them back in my bag. Monique looked up at the maitre d' and said cheerfully, 'Maybe you could get us the wine and a seafood platter, and we'll decide on the rest in just a bit.' He bowed slightly, and left.

'It's okay,' Monique said softly to the waiter.

'But, I don't understand…' Josh began to say, when Deven interrupted. 'He used to be at The Plaza earlier, right?'

The waiter nodded. 'So he was there when I had the heart attack. Just like the rest of you. But he didn't recognise me, like you didn't recognise him. So he didn't realise I wasn't…' he struggled a bit—he still found it difficult to accept that his untimely demise was an established fact '…I wasn't there,' he finished.

'Of course he didn't, poor man,' said Monique in motherly tones. She looked at the man's name tag. 'Ahmed, you've had a bad shock. I'd say you tell your boss you aren't feeling too good, and run along home. And don't worry, there's nothing wrong with you.' She slipped a couple of notes into his hand.

Ahmed nodded, and almost knocked Josh over in his hurry to get out of the alcove.

Next we had to deal with Varun, who was looking at all of us and wondering if the shrinks in Singapore offered volume discounts. Josh and Monique avoided catching his eye.

'Uhh, Varun, there's something I need to tell you…' I began. 'You remember my boss, Deven?'

He frowned. He'd never been too involved in my career. 'Think I met him once—fair short guy, bit of an asshole. Hang on—wasn't he the chap who popped it when you were in Singapore last?'

Deven scowled, and Monique looked upset.

'Well, he's here.'

'You mean he's buried here?'

I hesitated. 'No. It sounds pretty crazy, but his…ummm… ghost or something is here.'

'What crap!'

Monique butted in, 'Oh, but he is! And he's a really nice person once you get to know him…' Josh snorted, and Varun leaned back in his chair, looking amused.

'Maybe the spirit world changed him. Though I doubt it— once an asshole, always an asshole. So, you guys have been messing around with a planchette or something, have you?' He looked indulgent—like I said, he was a rationalist and didn't believe in ghosts, but he was too lazy to be rabid about it. Also, he was probably relieved that my sneaking off to meet Josh had such an innocently loony explanation.

Josh intervened. 'No, Varun, all three of us can see Deven. We think that it's because we were there when he died.'

'Cool, a group hallucination!' said Varun. 'I've heard of such things, but I haven't really come across it before. Where do you see this guy?'

'Um, he's right here?' said Josh.

Varun began to look a bit puzzled. 'You mean he's having dinner with us? What's he going to eat, virtual shrimps?'

'No, he's a vegetarian,' I said, a bit desperately. 'Look, Varun, I know it sounds crazy, but it's true. He's here, next to me.'

Varun suddenly lost his temper. 'Sanjana, you have to be the most credulous person I've ever met.' He got up and leaned over me 'Read my lips—there's no one here!'

I didn't reply. Varun gave a little exasperated exclamation, and turning away, took out a cigarette from his pocket. He fumbled with his lighter a little, and got it going, just as Deven rose from his chair exclaiming, 'I hate cigarettes.'

The flame from the lighter went through Deven's side as we watched, and his arm caught fire, burning with a ghostly flame that raged silently across his body. He thrashed and turned, flinging himself through Varun and onto the table. He was screaming in pain—it sounded so real, I couldn't understand how Varun and the other people in the restaurant couldn't hear him. It reminded me of a banned newsreel I had seen of students self-immolating after the Mandal Commission report. The flame was consuming him—his arm and part of his body shrivelled up and turned grey, and then vanished. His face was turned towards Monique, and it crumpled in agony as he gasped out—'Do something!' Monique made a strangled sound, and moved to help him, but by the time she got to her feet, he was gone. There was no trace of either him or the fire left. She sat back slowly, looking from Josh to me. Both of us were frozen to our chairs in horror.

Varun said, 'It's hot. See Sanjana, I told you there's no one here.'

'There isn't now,' said Monique in a strange voice, and went into violent hysterics.

We had to leave without having dinner. Josh took Monique home, and Varun and I grabbed a burger each at the McDonald's nearby. We walked slowly back to the hotel, and I tried to explain the events of the last few weeks to Varun. It was midnight by the time we reached our room.

Varun looked around, 'You don't still see him, do you?'

I shook my head. He sat down on the bed next to me, and hugging me, whispered into my hair 'I'm sorry if I've been insensitive. Is this why you've been, you know, a little unenthusiastic?'

I nodded, trying hard not to cry. Nothing had gone right since the wedding, and most of it was Deven's fault. For all I knew, Varun was wondering why he'd married me in the first place. I had been cranky, deceitful and frigid all through our so-called honeymoon. We'd had sex exactly twice since we got married, and it'd been a disaster both times.

'You're okay, now, right?' he said, turning my face up, and looking into my eyes.

'Yes,' I said.

'Don't you think we should make up for lost time?'

I nodded happily, and almost jumped on him in my eagerness to begin.

৪০৫৪

It's been a month since we returned to India, and my career and sex life are both back on track. I don't think I'll ever see Deven again (unless of course my sins pile up and I earn him as a boss in my next birth). But to be on the safe side, I threw away his copy of 'Blithe Spirit'. He was right anyway—the other two plays in the book weren't nearly as good.

৪০৫৪

AN UNLIKELY ACCOMPLICE

PARINDA JOSHI

A strange mix of citrusy fragrance infused with phenyl and medication made Brigadier Khanna's nostrils twitch and woke him up from the fangs of endless slumber. Something prevented his right eyelid from opening and it wasn't just the pounding headache. It felt like a paperweight balancing on his eyeball. He attempted to lift his right hand to yank out whatever was mounting pressure on his eye when he felt a whiplash, as if his wrist were chained to something. With a half-open eye, he tried to bring the blurred ceiling back into focus. Clean. White. Exempt from dangling fans. There was no hint of chipping paint on it. There were no destructive sounds of violence from the distance. No loud shrills from victims being tortured. No stench of urine, sweat or blood. He knew it right away. It wasn't what he'd suspected in his subconscious state.

There hadn't been a war. No war. No prisoner of war. No such luck. He'd die a war virgin.

Khanna tried to lift his head, but the pain in the back of his neck was immense. The dizzying effect of sedatives was perhaps wearing off.

'Wait wait. You'll injure yourself. Let me help you,' a mellow voice said. A face with clown curls blocked his view of the pristine ceiling. 'What do you need?'

'Who are you?' Khanna glowered.

'I'm Sister Jeannette.' *Nurse?* Clearly, something terrible had transpired. He blinked with one functioning eye and gave her face a good, appraising look. *Don't humour yourself, lady. Don't you go all pop queen on me with hair like Jeannette Jackson's and a voice like Bieber's.* She ignored his unspoken accusation and concentrated on the blood pressure monitor.

'Jeannette? Really? I'd have never guessed,' he scoffed. That trace of sarcasm brought some oxygen to his lungs. It made him feel confident in his body's ability to bounce back.

'Jeannette? Who's Jeannette? I said I'm Sister Janaki. You're in Karnavati hospital. Do you remember anything about last night?' she inquired, changing the intravenous drip, replacing it with a new bottle of colourless liquid.

'Just give me some Scotch, none of this nonsensical life-saving saline,' he grunted.

'Calm down. You're moving your hand too much. The drip needs to be stable. Do you remember last night?'

'Last night?' His eyes closed out of exhaustion. His ran his tongue sloppily to moisten his parched lips. 'Not particularly. But it'll come to me.'

'The doctor on duty will be in shortly. Are you a vegetarian?' she asked, promising him a meal, arranging the contents of a tray on the side table as was obvious from the clinking sound. Then she glided the curtains open. That cast a few harsh rays of sunlight on his lifeless face, jarring him slightly.

'Get me anything with a face.'

She shot him a derisive look. He watched her receding figure as she disappeared in the hallway. A bout of severe cough disoriented him for a while. The twitch of the two needles was increasingly uncomfortable and the occasional pain in his neck was excruciating.

The previous night slowly began flashing on the fleeting black film produced by facing the sun. He was in Manmohan's kitschy living room—munching on spiced cashews, discussing the unfolding of events, waiting for a report to come through. Manmohan was the Home Minister's personal assistant. Neat scotch lay on the side table for Khanna. Manmohan's right cheek was plump with the umpteenth piece of fried onion fritter ball nestled in it. Lalji—Manmohan's domestic help—was setting up dinnerware, his ears glued to their conversation.

There was a sudden stream of bullets on Manmohan's main door and windows facing the front yard sometime after nine o' clock. Khanna remembered being jolted with the unexpected assault, pulling out his handgun—the one he invariably carried—screaming at the unarmed others to escape via the kitchen. He recalled the front door immediately thrusting open, Lalji falling on his face, Manmohan lifting items in close proximity, hurling them at the attackers. Khanna's bullet had injured one of the infiltrators, knocking him down, while Manmohan tackled the other masked intruder. He recalled yelling at Lalji, asking him to help Manmohan and flee. 'Get the hell out of here. I'll handle these bastards.' His hands were fixated on the 9mm pistol, firing at the coward behind the couch. He'd waited for Manmohan and Lalji to escape through the kitchen before proceeding towards the bugger who was shooting like a child at a balloon shooter game. He remembered intense counter-firing. And then thump. Black out.

It troubled Khanna. He'd jeopardised their lives. Innocent, both of them. Their only blunder was lending him an ear. Khanna had to get up, find them.

'I understand you asked for a Scotch drip.' A doctor was at the door, a faint smile playing on his lips.

SIX WEEKS AGO...

Brigadier Khanna rolled out of bed, at three o' clock in the morning, slipped into a pair of jeans and a striped Polo T-shirt and hastily left his house. He jumped into his white Santro and slammed the accelerator. With one hand steady on the steering through the serene Cantonment establishment in Ahmedabad, he fervently attempted to call the number he'd received a text from minutes back. The phone faked incompetence. He tried it again. And again. They all went unanswered. It had been a disturbing text. 'Sonia in critical condition. Anand Villas, Farm House #20.' Another one had zoomed in seconds later. 'Your number was listed as emergency contact in her wallet.'

With the sweeping fear of impending bad news, Khanna tried to focus. On the dimly lit city streets, he drove as if he were driving a sports car, swerving, the screeching after-effect of his tires not registering on his anxious ears. The streets were soundless, with no foreshadowing of danger. An occasional truck zoomed past him, shaking his weightless car. A few young boys on bikes honked ceaselessly to draw attention to their boisterous selves. A weary cleaner or two swept the outsides of commercial buildings. Minutes later, he finally made it to the outskirts of the city. Bumpy, unpaved roads, lack of light posts and signboards made it tricky to navigate an area he wasn't familiar with. With no clear landmarks or directions, Khanna's stomach began to churn. GPS makers would blow their brains off before they could set it up in rural India, he'd often joke.

Khanna kept badgering the accelerator, his heart thumping, his mind consumed with Sonia's thoughts. His niece and all of nineteen, she was an architecture student, a state-level runner and had aced quizzes at the city level. A poised girl, with her head firmly on her shoulders, she was referred to as a role model for other kids in the family. He was her local guardian and she invariably informed him of all big and small outings despite being at the hostel on campus. How on earth did she land up in such a shady area, he wondered.

Khanna drove through countless farmhouses that served as the venue for shindigs of the Ahmedabadi elite.

Anand Villas, an oversized banner with an arrow proclaimed. It led to an uneven road flanked by trees on either side. About a kilometre into it, Khanna spotted numerous cars—Hondas, Tatas, BMWs; one of each variety parked haphazardly. He could see the flickering police car lights lit up the moonless sky. He finally pulled up in front of a sprawling mansion, the entrance sealed by yellow tape.

'I'm Brigadier Khanna. My niece, Sonia, is inside and I—' he fretfully attempted explanation, storming in.

One of the cops used his baton to impede Khanna. 'Can't go inside.'

'Look, my niece is here, in some trouble, God forbid.'

'Everyone here is in trouble, sir,' the man replied cheekily.

'What kind of nonsensical behaviour is this? I'm told she's in critical condition. Can you call the SHO or the Inspector?' Khanna tried to be dominant, his breath rising up to the neck like a rushing tornado.

'Name?'

'Sonia. Sonia Khanna.'

'*Ek* min, *wait kijiye.*'

It set his heart racing, his left hand covering his mouth, his right hand trembling in his pocket. Minutes later, another cop surfaced.

'*Aap mere saath aaiye.* Please come.'

'What the hell is happening here? Will someone please speak up?'

'Please follow me.' The cop, arguably a constable, started walking towards the ornate home, turning back to gesture with his hands.

Khanna followed, absorbing his surroundings. Three uniformed men were positioned at the gate guarding the sealed area. Several boys and girls were lined up against the towering compound walls, giving their statements. They all appeared to be in late teens or early twenties, decked up in high fashion; the girls in leg-baring outfits paired with heels and the boys in sports coats. Most of the girls were sobbing, whereas the boys wore long faces.

They walked swiftly all the way around the house on mosaic tiles that glittered in the dark. A makeshift dance floor jazzed up with LED lights stood unattended in one corner in the backyard. Massive speakers were placed at regular intervals, surrounding the dance floor. Blue string lights adorned Gulmohar trees that defined the boundaries of the lot. What must have been a party scene hours back was now a trashed version of it. Empty beer bottles, used cups, tissues, crates; all lay destroyed on the lush grass carpet. The tables with nibblers were intact. Two kneeled policemen were occupied with documenting evidences. The cop Khanna was following tapped another uniformed man on the back on his shoulder. The man turned to look at him.

'Sir, that girl—Sonia, her relative is here.'

Khanna scanned his uniform. The name tag read Inspector Jadeja.

'Father?' Jadeja solemnly asked, turning to Khanna.

'She's my niece, my elder brother's daughter. I'm her local guardian. For God's sake, will someone tell me where she is?'

'Your niece has been shot. She's been rushed to Bopal hospital.'

'What? How did she—shot? *Shot?* With a gun?'

'Unfortunately.'

That piece of information rendered Khanna speechless. Twenty-five years of training and experience with the Indian Army wasn't enough to face such an eventuality.

'That is abso—how bad is it? It better not be fatal,' Khanna said, rubbing his forehead with his sweaty palms.

'No details yet. She's in the ICU. That's actually where I'm headed.'

The perk of being in the army allowed him a ride in the jeep with Jadeja, who shared what might have transpired at the party. The Ahmedabad police had been religiously orchestrating a crackdown on all major farmhouses with a track record of liquor parties. Being a dry state, they had zero tolerance for those flouting rules. The investigators had lately been finding a huge stock of liquor and inebriated revellers from these parties where more than half the invitees were teens, Jadeja said.

'Such a nuisance. They're always up to something new. *Is baar toh hadd kar di.* The DJ brought in some Russian girls to perform fire-juggling stunts and God knows what else. Shameful,' Jadeja reported, shaking his head in disbelief. Khanna wasn't being an attentive listener, the anxiety of Sonia's injury numbing him.

'I still don't understand how Sonia was shot. Or what she was doing here in the first place.'

'Khannaji, from what we've gathered, an argument erupted between a guest and the party organiser. Led to a brawl. Sonia was somewhere in close proximity. When we raided the party, someone opened fire on us. Either the guest or the organiser—one of the two had a gun. She probably just got caught up in it.'

'What?' Khanna's stared at him slack jawed. 'Who are these people carrying guns?'

'The same ones who're trying to infuse drugs at these events. We found cocaine at the venue.'

Drugs? Guns? And his little Sonia caught up in it? At fifty-two, Khanna presumed he knew a thing or two about keeping a child safe. *How the heck had his angel gotten seeped into this mess?* She had spent the Saturday before the fateful day at his house helping him harvest red guavas and pomegranates from his backyard, making a tangy fruit salad, cheering for him when he hit appalling shots at the golf course. They had concluded the day with cold coffee and ice cream after which he'd dropped her off at her hostel. She was a second-year student. In two years, she'd be a trained architect. She wasn't like other kids her age; she didn't fancy movies or eating out or shopping or just chilling at popular hangout spots. Khanna often had to drag her out of campus and they would go watch a movie at the drive-in theatre. She would later complain about how it had turned out to be a colossal waste of time.

Sonia was an incorrigible workaholic. The only thing that got her excited outside of her course work were the Ahmedabad Architect Association events. She had been volunteering for them for a couple of years and hosted all their high-profile events frequently. She never missed inviting Khanna to these occasions. '*Chachu*, come *na*, you won't be bored, I promise,' she'd say chirpily.

Given the amount of time they spent together each week, he knew her intimately. This wasn't a place Sonia would have willingly gone to, that much he was certain of. Who had dragged her? What was their motive?

৪০৫৪

The jeep pulled up in front of the hospital. Khanna hurriedly walked alongside the cops. A constable waiting at the entrance saluted Jadeja, obsequiously filling him in. Panting, Khanna ran towards the inaccessible ICU and waited outside, scampering around in circles, hoping for someone to emerge from it and assure him that all was well with Sonia.

In between the fast approaching panic attacks, Sonia's entire life flashed in front of Khanna. The premature baby he'd carried in his arms soon after her birth had won him over instantly. She had breathing trouble when she was born, but her eyes were exceptionally sparkly and alert. One of the doctors had used vigilant in lieu of alert. Being the only girl child in their family, she was brought up like a princess. Gifted to him as a responsibility by his brother who was posted in Kochi. Shot at a party that had cocaine and alcohol. It was all too surreal and devastating. As soon as she was out of danger, he would get her transferred to the army hospital. Nothing short of the best treatment would do.

Minutes had passed. Perhaps hours. Eventually the ICU door swung open and two nurses carrying equipment walked out. Khanna scurried to the door that was left ajar. A doctor signing a stack of papers blocked his view of the bed. Khanna was about to knock on the door when the doctor stepped aside. And there it was—the horrific scene of Sonia's beautiful face being covered up by a white sheet. Khanna winced, momentarily losing all ability to process information. He ran up to her and snatched that fabric away, holding her fragile face in his helpless hands. Her eyelids sparkled from the makeup she wore. Her unsuspecting body lay there, cold and breathless. Her dreams, her promising future, her existence; all a thing of a past in a split second. Khanna held her tight, close to his heart, where she always had been, and wept like a child.

ഇ‌ലെ

A little past midnight, Khanna rose from his recliner, walked to the kitchen and poured himself some McDowell's. He'd undeniably turned into an insomniac and the strongest of whiskeys couldn't help. The guilt of failing as a guardian had thrown him into the dark recesses of throbbing agony, fury and failure.

In Brigadier Khanna's line of work, death came with the territory. The third Indo-Pak war had resulted in countless lives lost from his Kumaon regiment. The disgrace of being disqualified from combating due to a fractured spine had long played havoc on his psyche. He'd lost his parents shortly thereafter. The trail hadn't ended there. A few friends and family in other branches of Armed Forces had departed within quick succession owing to continued tension at the border. He'd survived it all. The snowballing list only made him more resilient.

But when he stood three feet away from the funeral pyre with Sonia's dainty body covered in white, thrust between the combustible heap, unruly flames hungrily leaping at her, burning every bit of her, his hands trembled vehemently. His body went numb. The wind fostering those flames cut through his heart. The sight of his elder brother collapsed by the side of the pyre next to his fainted wife only made it more excruciating.

When Khanna was capable of coherence, he held Sonia's white gold pendant with an engraved Shiva's image between his thumb and his forefinger, staring intently at the image, and made a promise to himself. He'd hunt down the bastard; the man who took Sonia's life.

৪০৫৫

The next rational step for Khanna was to involve an acquaintance, Manmohan Mehta, who was a PA to the Home Minister, Harikishan Bhatt. Khanna knew Manmohan through several government events where Khanna was often a guest of honour. Following up with the cops had led to police station rounds in an infinite loop. The Home Minister was the highest he could go in the hierarchy.

Bhatt was a polite middle-aged man sporting a goatee and the quintessential politician dress code—a white kurta-pajama accompanied by a charcoal khadi vest. Khanna walked into his clutter-free office at the Raj Bhavan in Gandhinagar. A peon shut the door behind Khanna.

'Very sorry to hear about your daughter, Khannaji.'

'My niece.'

'Right, my apologies. Tell me, how can I help?'

'Mr Bhatt, what has happened is unacceptable, unforgivable,' Khanna began, ignoring the lump that was forming in his throat. 'I'm not sure if you've been filled in on all the details. But shooting a teenage party doesn't just seem—'

'It wasn't just a teenage party. I just had a briefing with the commissioner. It was a rave. Cocaine, hashish, heroin; you name it.'

'And you're telling me this with a straight face? How are these things happening under your nose? What are the police doing?' Khanna asked, in an exasperated tone, seated on the edge of his chair.

Bhatt paused for a moment, then gently removed his bifocals and placed them on the table.

'I understand where you're coming from, Khannaji. A lot has changed in this city in the past few years.' He exhaled, his face melancholic. 'This is an enormous drug racket. You may have read about these parties in the papers. There have been a series of these going on in Goa, Mumbai, Kolkata and several other cities. Ahmedabad is the new entrant it seems.'

'And what exactly have the cops done to stop this?'

'They have been launching a crackdown on all such parties. But this is all very recent.'

'Look, Mr Bhatt, all I want to know is who shot Sonia. She hated parties. She did not belong to that party.

There's a lot more than meets the eye here,' Khanna said emphatically, banging his fist on the table.

'The police are working very hard on getting to the bottom of this. I am giving you my word. We shall have the details very soon.'

Khanna shifted in the chair uncomfortably, his breath caught up in his chest.

Bhatt stiffened and leaned in a little. 'You please don't worry. I'll make sure we make some key progress in a few days. I'll personally call you.'

๛

With uneventful days systematically giving way to futile weeks, Khanna was slowly but surely turning into a non-believer. He wasn't built to rely on others in any case. When realisation dawned, he wasted no time in scouting for potentially useful information that could lead to clues. The police repeatedly came back with status quo but the young boys in Cantonment and his neighbour's stoner son, Neil, in particular, had given him a unanimous answer. *Hollywood.*

'I can't do it, uncle. I've never done it before,' Neil asserted, his feet up on the bean bag in his bedroom.

'You bloody well can. Don't give me that puppy face. You've been doing it for years.' With his self-absorbed college-going appearance replete with funky hair and graphic tee, Neil fit the 'ideal consumer' image down to a tee.

'Shh uncle, you'll get me killed. Dad is outside in the corridor.' Neil sprinted towards the door to lock it, then leaned against it, puffing.

'I suppose you wouldn't want me to share with him that I've seen you and your useless gang roll joints practically every other night on the terrace.'

'Please don't. Please. Dad will slaughter me.' Niel looked petrified.

'What's bothering you?'

'I—we buy from this dude, Benny, who sells stuff right around here behind the mess. I've never actually bought it from elsewhere. Never alone, in any case.'

'Benny?'

'Benny Machado. College dude. Does small-time business just around here.'

'Hmm,' Khanna evaluated that piece of information. 'Why isn't Benny on our list of people who can potentially provide clues?'

'That's what I'm trying to tell you. Benny knows nothing. He is an insignificant player. He always tells us that he gets all his stock from Hollywood.'

Khanna thought about it for a moment. 'Okay then, Hollywood it is. And you're going to do it for me.'

'Uncle!'

'I'm with you. You just have to bait this reseller. That's it.'

'What if I get caught?'

'Oh, grow a pair. And do as I say.'

The stretch between University cross roads and Gulbai Tekra was home to numerous shacks. It was a rare slum in prime real estate nestled between engineering colleges and luxury residential area, ironically named Hollywood. The slum dwellers had set up a primary business of creating idols of deities—from pocket charms to life-sized ones made from plaster of Paris. The surrounding streets often brimmed over with vehicles atop which deities and mortals coexisted.

The next afternoon, Khanna dropped Neil at Hollywood and waited in his car inconspicuously. A couple of eager souls tried selling Neil handicrafts when he asked for *asli maal*. Some scanned him suspiciously. A seemingly vulnerable boy pointed Neil to a hut deep in the heart of the slum. 'Look for Sanjay,' the boy advised.

Neil walked gingerly through constricted, fetid lanes flanked by garbage and water bodies, unclothed children running around, dispersed groups of elderly men and women with their heads covered, idly seated on the treacherous porches, some smoking beedis, others chewing on a twig, boys playing cricket, music blaring from electricity-challenged huts.

After much asking around for Sanjay, Neil was outside the treasure shack. A gentle knock on the door educed no response. Eventually, a lanky boy wearing a torn *ganji* and tattered jeans emerged, his eyes heavy and swollen.

'Yes?'

'Do you know Benny? Benny Machado?'

With that name dropping, Sanjay looked at ease but didn't respond.

'I, umm, need some, you know, stuff.'

'Charas *ya* ganja?' Sanjay asked mechanically.

'What else do you have?' Neil put up a brave front.

'Tell me what you need. I'll arrange for it.' Sanjay was emaciated, smelled like a weed factory and his front teeth were decomposed.

'Assorted drugs. Ecstasy. Marijuana. Whatever else you can arrange. It's for my birthday bash.'

'How many people? When?'

Neil put his hands in his pockets and straightened his back once the basic information exchange had happened. 'Do you have the stock here? Let me see what you have.'

'Boss, don't worry. I'll arrange for it.'

'So you don't!'

'*Arre* sir, you please don't worry.'

'Look, if you can't share details I'll find someone else. I don't think you can handle it in any case.' Khanna had made him practice delivering the ultimate threat.

'Don't lose your cool, sahib. There's a big distributor of designer drugs. Will send one or two boys at the party with mixed samples. Need 50 per cent advance.'

'Benny? Please.' Neil scoffed. 'He hasn't had good stock

in a while. My friend got so many infections from his last batch of ecstasy.'

'That Benny is a *haraami*. He buys from me and doesn't pay on time. He's no distributor. I'm talking about a big one.'

'You all say that. Benny called you a big distributor. Ha.' Neil faked laughter, a shiver running down his spine. 'Who is this big distributor?'

'*Naam ka kya karna hai,* sahib. Why get into that? Supplies are guaranteed.'

'*Dekh* bhai, I don't have time for this. I don't trust fly-by-night operators. Had enough of those.' With that, Neil turned to walk away.

'Wait. Wait. Not a fly-by-night operator. He's a biggie. Raghav Reddy. You must have read about him in papers. He supplies to all the parties in Ahmedabad.'

That was all the information Neil was after. He created a fuss over the cost and left.

৩৩৪

Khanna launched a comprehensive web search on his phone on his drive back. It had been quick to dispense results. Raghav Reddy was linked with Tenali Cartel. As soon as he dropped Neil off, Khanna located a discreet area and dialled a Delhi number.

'Bhatnagar, Khanna here. You have a few minutes?'

Bhatnagar was a dear friend and had an office on the

topmost floor of Sena Bhavan in Delhi where the Indian Army's Military Intelligence operated from. The building was the closest India got to the Pentagon. Its tunnel of corridors and cramped offices helped India's military spies maintain a layer of anonymity. They'd spent five years together when Khanna was posted in Delhi.

'Hey hey, Scotch Doc,' Bhatnagar responded with marked enthusiasm. 'Still a double bogey player?' Khanna needed no reminders of his disastrous golf game.

'I'm well. Listen, I need some intelligence on Raghav Reddy. Drug Lord. Heads Tenali Cartel. I want to know his connection to Ahmedabad.'

'Cartel?' Bhatnagar laughed heartily. 'Since when did out-of-work oldies start messing with drug lords?'

'Bhatnagar, please. It's urgent. And personal.'

'Okay, okay. Don't whine. I'll see what I can find.'

∞

Time had become inconsequential. Nothing new had surfaced from the police investigation. No arrests. No key facts. No clarity on Sonia's murder. Status quo ruled. The rage Khanna felt couldn't be suppressed. It manifested itself everywhere; with the domestic help, with his colleagues, with stray onlookers.

One day a headline hit Khanna in the gut. 'Teen girl raped at a rave party in Kolkata.' Fury rushed through his veins threatening to explode them. He scanned the details.

A familiar name popped up, a monstrous laugh filling up Khanna's space from the newspaper, or so he felt. *Raghav Reddy*. He tried to hold the anger in his fist but could no longer contain it. Khanna had to do something. Take matters in his own hands. He had to take Reddy down somehow. And for that, he needed to know about Reddy.

Days later, Bhatnagar circled back with information on Reddy.

'I'll fax you a detailed report but listen to this. This Reddy guy is a different beast.' Bhatnagar kicked off the introduction dramatically. 'He heads up South East Asia's largest drug trafficking organisation, Tenali Cartel. He even has a nickname, Chota Reddy, for his short stature.' Bhatnagar giggled like a schoolgirl. 'Let me see what else. Ah—' he continued with striking eagerness, reading from what Khanna presumed was a bulky printout glorifying Reddy's life.

'Hello?'

'I'm listening.'

'Okay okay. So Reddy became India's top drug kingpin in 2003 after the arrest of his rival Kafi Ali of the Gulf Cartel. Forbes estimated his net worth to be roughly US $1 billion. They also called him the "biggest drug lord of all time from South East Asia".'

Khanna tried to absorb the information, his brows furrowed, his legs crossed in his *baithak* in the veranda.

'Tenali Cartel smuggles multi-ton cocaine shipments from

Turkey through Sri Lanka to India and has distribution cells throughout India.'

'Where are they based?'

'Hyderabad. The organisation has also been involved in the production, smuggling and distribution of methamphetamine, marijuana, and heroin.'

'Is there anything about Ahmedabad?'

'Ah, now this is interesting. And funny too. Sources disagree on the date of birth of Reddy, with some stating he was born—'

'Bhatnagar, listen, I need names of his contacts in Ahmedabad.'

'*Arre sun le* yaar. He sold bananas as a child in Tenali. His father was supposedly an agriculturist but it is believed that he also grew opium poppy. His sisters—'

Bhatnagar narrated the useful and the useless at the speed of light. At the end of that exhausting report, Khanna could hear him guzzling down a barrel of water. Some things never change.

'Thanks for that essay, Bhatnagar. I know I'll ace the 'Know Your Criminals' subject in school this year. *Chal*, we'll talk later.'

'Funny! *Accha* listen, did you ask for his Ahmedabad connection?'

'That's the *only* thing I asked for.'

'There's a reference here. Benny, it says. Benny Machado.

Runs Reddy's Gujarat operations. But this report is slightly dated.'

Benny? Benny-Neil's-supplier Benny? Benny-who-sells-drugs-at-Cant Benny? Why hadn't it occurred to Khanna to corner Benny? He'd alluded to it but that duffer Neil had underplayed Benny's reach, calling him a nobody. Benny spearheaded Reddy's Gujarat operations! If he ran the operations, he might have been at the party where Sonia was shot. At the very least, Benny's men would have been there. He must have known something, anything. Khanna could see the bull's eye. He had to get Benny somehow.

೩೦೦೩

One chilly Friday night, Neil had been briefed by the cops. All he had to do was bait Benny and pretend to buy from him.

Neil had resisted vehemently, 'Uncle, we rarely see Benny nowadays. Girlfriend trouble, his sidekick said. She is sick or in the hospital or something.'

'Find a way, Neil. Make it happen.' Khanna pushed Neil to somehow get Benny to meet him once.

Neil was as scared as a puppy at a dogfight, but Khanna assured him that his secret was safe. The scene was scripted well, scoped out and the entire set up had been meticulously planned. Khanna had involved Manmohan and Bhatt, so the cops wouldn't drop the ball. Half a dozen plain-clothed policemen surrounded the area behind the canteen at Cantonment just after eight o' clock at night.

As per the plan, Neil headed out towards the back of the mess, his face covered in his hoodie, a distinct hesitation in his gait. There was a slight nip in the air and a hazy white blanket of fog scattered the diffused light from the many lampposts. Minutes later, Benny showed up on a motorcycle, a lit cigarette in his mouth. He looked around cautiously, then walked up to Neil, silently acknowledging Neil's presence with a nod.

Khanna gave Benny a closer look from his hideout. Benny had a chiselled face, an intense look and he walked with the aura of an intellectual. He wore a checked shirt, scruffy jeans, sported a stubble and his messy hair had yellow streaks, Khanna could tell even in the dimmed light. The diamond stud in his left ear sparkled under the streetlight. Benny cut the profile of a fashionable youngster, not a drug dealer. It took Khanna by surprise.

Minutes later, easily enough, out came the packet from Benny's jacket and so did the cops from their hideouts.

ॐ

While the cops worked on eliciting information from Benny, Khanna had business to take care of. Benny was just a tiny piece of the puzzle.

Over the next few days Khanna pulled every business card worth its salt that he had. Ministers, top cops, CBI superstars, anti-narcotics cell officials, ex-army chiefs, journalists, activists; if they were influential, Khanna had a hot line set up with them. Mobilising powerful people was the only way he could take on a drug lord of Reddy's stature. He woke up with a single crucial goal each morning; to create tremendous pressure on the authorities about Reddy. No connection was too big or too small. If wasn't as if there was no push back but Khanna persevered. Interviews of victims' families, exposés at the grass roots level, extensive media coverage that spoke to the middle class; it was a massive, concentrated effort.

It must have been good karma, for soon enough the phone rang.

'Khannaji, I have news.' Manmohan spoke in a high-pitched voice. 'That bastard Benny has opened his mouth finally.'

'What did he say?'

'The commissioner has a meeting with Mr Bhatt this evening. I will try to get some details on this case as well. Why don't you come home later tonight? I'll try to get my hands on a copy of the report by then.'

Khanna recalled that invitation from Manmohan distinctly. And then that stream of bullets at his house…

BACK TO THE PRESENT DAY…

The young doctor with gelled hair checked Khanna's reports, then his pulse, then the back of Khanna's ear, his eyes narrowed. 'Your stitches look good. The fever hasn't shot up in the past six hours. And your pulse is back to normal. How is the pain?'

'As all pains are. Stupefying, but I'll survive.'

The doctor smirked. 'This calls for a scotch drip.'

Khanna shot him a perfunctory smile.

'I'm glad this civilian hospital has been able to score.' The doctor promised a rendezvous later in the evening and left.

The soothing effects of sedatives had worn off and Khanna's memory had made a whooshing comeback. It brought along a fit of rage and anxiety about Manmohan. A gentle knock on the door made Khanna look up. It was the Home Minister.

'Mr Bhatt?' Khanna attempted to sit up.

'Please, please. Settle down, Khannaji.'

'I wasn't expecting...is everything okay?'

'Manmohan has been admitted to this hospital as well. Came to visit him and learnt you were right here.'

'I've been very worried about him,' Khanna groaned.

'He's fine, luckily,' Bhatt assured, making himself comfortable on a flimsy plastic chair, his glasses hanging from a cord around his neck.

Khanna breathed a sigh of relief. 'I'm still in denial about the attack.'

'So are we,' Bhatt concurred, stroking his goatee. 'Reddy has a solid network. He's got men everywhere. Only that can explain the attack at Manmohan's house.' Then, for effect, he added, 'Investigation is underway.'

Those three words again; the ones Khanna had come to despise severely.

'Anyway,' Bhatt said, 'you must get some rest. Good to know you're recovering. I will check on you again in a few days. *Mere layak kuch kaam ho toh bataiyega zaroor.*' He folded his hands in the archetypal politician manner and got up to take Khanna's leave.

'Thank you,' Khanna almost let Bhatt off, then a light bulb went off in his head. 'Mr Bhatt?'

'Yes?'

'Manmohan mentioned last night that Benny has given his statement. You wouldn't have any information on it, would you?'

Bhatt looked away, his eyes blinking rapidly. 'Let's talk when you get home. Okay?'

'Do you have—did you read the report?'

'I had a briefing on it this morning.'

'And?'

Bhatt looked outside the window for a few seconds, as if contemplating, then spoke in a restrained manner, 'You probably haven't seen the papers this morning. The news of a crackdown on Reddy's empire is splashed across countless newspapers. Narcotics worth crores have been seized, two dozen perpetrators have been arrested and a special committee has been set up to aid the anti-narcotics cell in the matter. Reddy, of course has gone absconding. But this is a good start, Khannaji.'

Despite exceptional efforts to push it through, the outcome about Reddy brought Khanna no solace whatsoever.

'I meant about Benny.' His hunger to learn the truth was turning insatiable by the minute.

Bhatt paused tepidly, his hands in his vest pockets, then said, 'So this Benny guy was involved in a tussle that night with the party organiser at Anand Villas.'

The lingering pain only aggravated Khanna's impatience.

'The police suspect that both Benny and the organiser had discovered that they were working for Reddy while coaxing the party-goers into signing up for their model of propagating drugs,' Bhatt spoke, unperturbed.

'The what?'

'Reddy had this signature model. It is the next big thing for youngsters to do after the call centre way of making a quick buck,' Bhatt said, drawing an unsettling analogy. 'Anyway, both boys had locked horns. Given that they were under the influence, a fight had broken out and the organiser happened to be armed.'

'That's a great story, but how the heck did Sonia land up there?' Bhatt lost patience every time someone attempted to provide insight because ultimately they all went off on a tangent.

'Khannaji, this Reddy has sort of emerged as a true entrepreneur, expanding his business to the middle class.'

'I still don't see the connection.'

'See, drugs in this country have remained a passion of the rich and a pastime of hostellers. This man seems to have pitched a modified Amway model to the middle class boys and girls. The boys are lured by get-rich-quick schemes and the girls, glamorous lifestyles. His victims are his biggest supporters and propagators.'

'What does Sonia have to do with all this?' Khanna couldn't help yelling. Why did people go on incessantly with monologues about entirely extraneous matters?

'Please, settle down Khannaji. Don't stress yourself.'

'Then tell me in a way I can understand.' Infuriated, he stretched out each word.

'Reddy had a distinct model for the girls. It wasn't just making money off of coaxing people into buying drugs. That wouldn't have been motivation enough for girls who came from simple God-fearing backgrounds. They had a different reward system. Fulfilment of goals came with free passes for everything from these fashion weeks that happen in metros to Bollywood premiers to front row seats at concerts.'

'What rubbish,' Khanna rebuked. 'And you call this detailed reports? Sounds like a B-grade movie script.'

'Khannaji, I can understand your pain.'

'No, you don't. Because you're not telling me anything that I need to hear.'

It was all too sophisticated to be run by an illiterate drug-seller. Khanna was still unconvinced about the money-making model. But it had nothing to do with Sonia.

'It's complicated, Khannaji. And your health is fragile. Let's meet this Sunday and I'll tell you all about it.'

'I don't understand this hocus-pocus. What are you alluding to?' The conversation and the premonition of something terrible were making Khanna groggy.

'Nothing. I'm alluding to nothing.'

'Bhattji, do me this favour and just give it to me straight. I deserve to know.' Khanna rose from the bed, the saline drip swinging on the side. The needle twitched under his skin, eliciting a gasp from him.

'Nothing will come out of this. She is already dead,' Bhatt said gravely, then placed a comforting hand on Khanna's shoulder, not making eye contact.

'I consider you a friend, Mr Bhatt. You know what has happened. You owe me that information. I deserve to—' Another bout of cough disoriented him.

'Let it be, Khannaji.' Bhatt's face was stoic.

'*Let it be?* I've been spending every wretched moment in the hope that I'll learn the truth one day. The truth about who murdered my Sonia. You're telling me the truth is out and I don't deserve to know? What the hell is the matter? What are you trying to cover up? And who are you trying to protect? A bloody murderer? A drug lord? Do these people own a handful of politicians now…or the entire ministry?'

Bhatt whizzed past the bed towards Khanna, his index finger pointed towards him. 'You think I'm covering up?' he demanded, seething, his face red. 'What do you want me to tell you? That that guy Benny wasn't alone in this? That your niece wasn't innocently dragged into it? *That she herself was actively involved in it?*'

'How dare you slander her? Have the politicians stooped so low that they are out to malign innocent dead people instead of thriving criminals?'

Bhatt screamed at someone waiting outside Khanna's room. 'Get me the Anand Villas shooting case report. *Jaldi.*' Then he turned to Khanna. He looked like someone on the verge of getting a stroke. 'Okay, here is the truth. She worked alongside Benny on this.'

'Who? Sonia?'

'Yes, Sonia.'

'*Sonia and Benny? Did you say Sonia and Benny? Bakwaas band kijiye aap.* And please leave.'

'According to Benny's statement, his *girlfriend,*' Bhatt emphasised that last word, 'Sonia, was trying to pull him away from the fight that erupted between the organiser and him, when the bullet pierced through the left part of her neck.'

'Mr Bhatt, I'm warning you, please leave before I—' Khanna was livid, his body trembling. Two nurses came running in and tried to hold him from either side. That didn't discourage Bhatt from spilling the beans.

'He was a fourth-year architecture student. They had been in a relationship since two years, as per the confirmation from her classmates.'

A million things inside Khanna shattered. The pain was palpable, paralysing, ultimate, like nothing he had experienced before.

A young man returned promptly with a file. Bhatt grabbed it and tossed it at Khanna. He began to storm out, then arbitrarily stopped, turned to look Khanna in the eye, and said, 'That is the bitter truth. Can you handle it? We don't know our own children. Such are the pitiable times we live in.' Bhatt inhaled loudly, then continued his assault. 'It is true, Khannaji, Sonia wasn't just a victim. She was a propagator.'

৪০৫৪

THE U-TURN

ATULYA MAHAJAN

'Honey, I think we need to rush to the hospital. RIGHT NOW!'

Anmol looked up from his desk at his pregnant wife Komal, gasping in pain, barely able to stand, a hand on her bulging stomach. Her face was pale and sweaty, her long hair dishevelled. She seemed a far cry from the glamorous goddess she once used to be.

'B...b...but,' he stammered, 'we are still a month away from your due date.'

'Damn you, Anmol! Hurry up. This pain is killing me.' Her voice was hoarse, a mix of pain and frustration. It was two o' clock in the night. She had been trying to go to sleep for a few hours now, but the pain just kept getting worse. The family gynaecologist, Dr Preeti, had said that the due date is always tentative, and ultimately it is nature's decision when to pop the baby. She had asked them to be prepared starting three weeks from the date, but even that would be a week from now. This may very well be a false alarm, but there was only one way to find out.

'Let's go, Anmol,' she shouted, as Anmol took an extra few seconds to shut down his laptop, still in the midst of the presentation he was preparing for his CEO, to be delivered the next morning.

Anmol sighed as he rushed to grab the emergency bag prepared for this day, but realised that they hadn't got down to doing it, never anticipating this early arrival. He quickly filled the bag with one of her gowns, a towel, the medical file, and a picture of them lounging in a beach chair from last year's Thailand trip. The doctor had recommended keeping a happy picture to help her relax during the ordeal.

He grabbed her hand, led her down the flight of stairs, seated her in the car, and rushed to lock their apartment in the suburbs of Bengaluru, where they had moved two years ago, after spending a few years in the US. Anmol worked as a senior manager at a leading technology company and was eyeing a lucrative promotion to Director.

He had not been too happy earlier in the year when Komal announced that her pregnancy test was positive. He had made her take a second one, just to be sure. He had taken *precautions*. It was not possible. This was too early. These were the golden years of his career. There was the promotion to Director, which would take him ahead of anyone in his peer group. There was the trip to Europe they had planned as a reward for the inevitable promotion. This was not a time for him to be running around a baby, trying to change diapers, cleaning poop, being soaked in fresh pee.

He returned to the car after locking the doors of the apartment, still dressed in his night clothes, but carrying a shirt and trousers.

'Sit tight, Komal. We'll be at the hospital in twenty minutes and you'll be fine.' He caressed her sweaty forehead, as she sat next to him grunting, gasping for breath.

'Just drive. Go.' Her voice was a whisper now.

He turned on the ignition of his Toyota Fortuner and the heavy SUV came to life. The Beast, she called her. He called her The Hulk. This car was one of his prized possessions, a symbol of his journey up the corporate ladder. He had bought her last year after his promotion to senior manager. The big bonus that came that year for delivering one of the biggest projects the firm had undertaken in recent times had helped. He was leaving his peers far behind, just like The Beast did on the road. The roads would be clear at this time of the night, so he wasn't too worried about traffic. However, her condition seemed bad. He just hoped she'd be under the care of a doctor soon.

He called up his sister from his phone. She lived in Delhi with her husband and two children, Pari and Parag. Pari was six and Parag three. Anmol had not seen them when they were born, since he had been busy toiling in the US, and in the last two years since the return, he had only met them once last year, at Parag's second birthday. Even then, he had been wary of Pari's ice-cream dripping onto his Canali suit or Parag pooping in his arms, while their doting parents ran around, tending to guests, bringing what seemed like an endless line of bottle after bottle of milk, changing diapers, comforting them, eating their leftover food, not having a single relaxed moment while they ensured that the children were fully taken care of.

The phone rang for a minute before being picked up. In his nervous stupor, he hadn't realised that she must be sleeping at this late hour. Not that it mattered. He couldn't handle it alone. He needed help. Mom and dad just had to choose this time to go on a trek to Kailash Mansarovar. Their being home would have been such a big help. He was clueless alone.

His sister's voice crackled on the phone. 'What? The labour has started? But wasn't she due in a month? *Chal* don't worry, children are God's gifts. They don't come via FedEx that you will know exactly when they will arrive. Take care of Komal. Stay with her. Keep her relaxed. More importantly, you also stay relaxed. Take leave from office for a month and tend to your family. Work can wait.'

Anmol couldn't help laugh, waking Komal from her semi-sleepy state. A month's leave meant certain career-suicide for him. He would not get that promotion. Somebody else who could work harder and longer would come along, and everybody would forget Anmol. He might as well jump from the top of their forty-floor apartment complex.

'What's so funny?' Komal asked, a hand gingerly placed on her stomach. The pain had eased up somewhat.

'Nothing, baby.' He kept a hand on her forehead, comforting her. The hospital was still ten minutes away. 'Soon we'll be at the hospital and you'll be alright.'

'Did you find out if they'll allow you in the delivery room? In the US, they allow fathers inside. I wouldn't mind holding on to your hand while the baby tears up my insides.'

'No, baby. They don't. India works very differently from the US. They won't let anyone inside. But don't worry. The doctors will take good care of you.'

He was lying. He hadn't bothered to find out. Even if they permitted, there was no way he could get himself to do it. He was worried about passing out himself, which wouldn't help matters at all. Besides, he planned to make a quick trip to the office while she was in the hospital. He had to complete that presentation. Even if he couldn't actually meet the CEO the next morning, he wanted to be able to send the slides and hope to be excused for not making it to the meeting. The CEO was a finicky man who had once fired one of his assistants because he was wearing a red tie, the colour he abhorred, as it reminded him of his unfaithful ex-wife. Nobody at work had worn red after that day.

Anmol would see off Komal into the labour room, change into work clothes and rush to the office, which was luckily located not too far from the hospital. He'd get his work done and be back before the baby came out.

'I am scared,' she said, holding on to his hand as he steered the car with the other one. 'Promise me that you will be there for me.'

'Of course, Komal. I'll be right there. We are in it together. Everything will be fine.' He said, keeping an eye on the road, driving carefully to avoid any potholes.

'Thanks, baby. I love you.'

'I love you too, sweetie.'

To say that Anmol was scared would be an understatement. Going by what he had seen and heard so far, raising a baby was no child's play, and he was terrified. Ever since news of his wife being pregnant had spread in the office, people had been sharing advice with him.

'Make sure you baby-proof your house. You wouldn't imagine how the most innocuous of things can be a hazard for little babies. If it is something they can put in their mouth, they will do it. If it has a hole in it, they will stick a finger in. You can't have any exposed electricity sockets. You can't have any mosquito repellent or rat poison in sight. Make sure you sterilise anything that gets in contact with the baby. Make sure there is no glass object that can break and cause harm.' This had gone on for months now. What resounded in Anmol's ears was 'Make sure you don't expect to have a life anymore…'

Yadav from the finance vertical had his own story to add. 'Make sure you don't buy any local toys. They have lead in the paint. One of my neighbours had a child who developed an allergy to wheat all of a sudden. The doctors said sometimes lead can cause such conditions. Kids these days have the strangest of diseases. You can just never be too careful.'

Yadav was just jealous of his success. Five years older to him and still languishing at the manager level, mysteriously happy in his mediocrity. Anmol couldn't understand what he kept smiling about while leading his miserable existence. *Maybe he had also inhaled some lead as a child.* Nothing else explained his happiness with his life. *He did keep talking fondly of his children, but how could his son learning karate or daughter playing the guitar make him so happy?* Anmol couldn't care less about Yadav, that loser of a man. He had even rejected taking on a massive project last year as it would involve a lot of travel, and he wanted to be close to his family. That project would have got him promoted to Senior Manager, but the idiot didn't want it. Anmol rolled his eyes thinking about him.

Yadav or no Yadav, Anmol was terrified of what was going to happen. He was reminded of scenes from movies where death row convicts were being walked to the gallows. Soon he would be a father. In a few years, he would be doing the rounds of schools, begging for his child to be admitted, and then pay as much in fees as the amount he used to make in a year when he started his career. He or she would perhaps go on to have affairs. They'd probably sneak out of school for a romantic liaison or two. Hopefully no MMSes would be made and sent out on the Internet to the eternal shame of the family.

Anmol had sacrificed a lot to get to this position. He had slogged like a pig, working weekends, staying up late, sometimes working overnight in the office, just so his bosses could be happy. When people were busy gossiping about the cricket team or the latest Salman Khan movie over hour-long lunches in the cafeteria, he had eaten lunch at his desk every single day. When people went out to watch movies or to shake a leg on Friday nights, he had stayed in the office, working on presentations and business cases. Now so close to his target, he felt like it had been a lost cause.

Komal had been obstinate. They had discussed waiting for later, but she wouldn't even hear the a-word. She had also been a career woman, strong, confident, eager to grow. But now she was willing to drop everything and take a long leave from work to be a mother. His parents too were excited to become grandparents to another child, and Anmol had no choice but to play along. His fears and concerns had gone unheard, but he had lived in terror the last eight odd months. Not that it had stopped him from continuing to spend long nights in the office. Komal hadn't complained much, trying her best to manage as well as she could.

Parenting was going to change everything. He would no longer be able to go to those lovely beach resorts. Instead they'll have to hunt travel websites for 'family-friendly' resorts that had play-areas, kiddie pools and high-chairs at the restaurant. The occasional glass of wine he used to enjoy would be out of question; now he would be busy requesting milk bottle refills.

He wondered what all of this would do to his relationship with Komal. Their love-life was pretty much finished already, so it probably couldn't get much worse. He was reminded of a family function they had attended last year where one of his cousin sisters had a massive argument with her husband over something he said or did to their baby. Perhaps it was that he gave the child a glass of Pepsi to drink and she freaked out at him for being so irresponsible. He couldn't remember the details, but it had been embarrassing to watch. He had heard many people say that children did this to couples who would start off arguing, move on to sleeping in different rooms, and eventually become strangers to each other and drivers to their kids.

They were at the hospital. Komal was calmer now. The staff at the Emergency efficiently ushered her to the maternity ward on a stretcher, where the doctor on duty examined her as Anmol waited outside, walking about the corridor, taking breaks to check his BlackBerry for any new emails from the US team.

He noticed a little child nearby, sitting in the lap of an older lady, perhaps his grandmother. The boy was maybe three or four years old; Anmol couldn't really tell. He was very patiently looking on, watching his father running around, getting admission formalities done for his wife. The boy was going to get a sibling, and seemed rather excited.

Intrigued, Anmol sat down on a bench close to where they were seated.

'Daadi, when will the baby come?'

'Very soon, *beta*. Don't you want to sleep now? It is so late.'

'I don't want to sleep Daadi. I want to meet mommy. I want to see the baby.'

His *daadi* smiled and kissed him on his head as he clung to her tightly, like a kangaroo baby secure with his mother. She started singing a lullaby to him. Five minutes later, Anmol could hear him snoring, deep in slumber, his teeny fingers clasped around his grandmother's arms.

He had to wait for the doctor's update before he could head to the office to get his work done. Bored, he sat in front of the TV, hoping for some entertainment. He hadn't watched television in ages. At one time he used to watch the occasional comedy show like *Friends* or *30 Rock*, but he had given that up long ago. TV was just a silly waste of time that could be better used securing new projects for the company and getting ahead of his peers in the rat race.

They were showing a music reality show on the television. A six-year-old boy was singing melodies originally sung by veterans of the Bollywood music industry, with no sign of stage fright or lack of self-confidence. Anmol's thoughts went back to a debate he had contested in school as a teenager. He had got so nervous that his voice had started faltering and he had forgotten half of the speech he had painstakingly memorised, much to the amusement of the assembled audience. His classmates had teased him for that fiasco for the entire year. This boy was a prodigy of some sort.

He wasn't the only one. One after the other, the show featured equally talented young boys and girls. Interspersed with their performances were shots of their anxious parents watching on as their progeny sang with effortless ease. Amazingly, the children looked relaxed while the parents seemed jittery, ready to burst into tears at a moment's notice.

Was this going to be his life? He knew his sister used to talk of starting some activity classes for Pari and Parag. *Was he going to become this parent who shuttled his child from one class to the next, in a never-ending competition to make the child win contests and leave others behind?*

The door of the ward opened and the doctor came outside looking for Anmol, still watching TV intently.

'Congrats, Anmol. Komal is indeed in labour. You're going to be a dad soon.' The words hit Anmol like a cold slab of ice. He suddenly felt dizzy. *This was it.*

'Don't you worry. She is fine and in good hands. For now, she is comfortable. We don't know when the delivery will happen, but there is time. God knows, could be as long as twelve hours. You should make yourself comfortable and get some rest, because she will need your support soon.'

The good doctor Priya patted his shoulder as she left. Thirty years ago, she had likely done the same to his father when she delivered Anmol. Anmol wondered if his father had felt the same emotions he was feeling right now.

They were now showing a commercial on television, featuring an anxious mother watching her daughter shooting basketball hoops unsuccessfully, egging her on, keeping a close eye on her failures, her severe face reflecting disappointment and sending a message that the girl wasn't going to get out of the court till she managed it. Anmol sighed.

Unable to watch any more of the depressing TV, he whipped out his phone and started browsing Facebook. He hadn't talked to any of his old buddies in many years but thanks to Facebook and LinkedIn, he knew exactly who was where and at what role. He had been one among the pack at college, but broken out in his own league in the professional space. Today he was making more money than any of his classmates. He was married to Komal, who was prettier than any of their wives. He was the topper now.

Anmol started going over his Facebook time line. One of his colleagues who got married last week and was currently on his honeymoon had shared some pictures. Him and the bashful wife having lunch together. Him and the wife snorkelling together. Him and the wife in a private pool in their suite together. Luckily, no pictures of him and the wife doing you-know-what together. Anmol checked out all the photos. She was hot, but not hotter than Komal, even though she hadn't been particularly sexy in the last few months.

Then there was a picture that Yadav had uploaded. It was his daughter holding up a picture she had drawn of the family, with a caption saying, 'Look at the beautiful picture my four-year-old daughter drew of her family. We should change her name to Picasso.' Anmol smirked. The painting was terrible. Where there should be faces were poorly scribbled shapes, there seemed to be no sense of symmetry, Yadav was drawn with only one leg and his wife had a moustache. Twenty people had liked it already with comments gushing over the creative genius of the child.

Anmol added a comment saying, 'LOL Yadav ji, looks like you broke a leg :-P.'

His time line was sprawling with updates about babies. Someone had become a parent and posted pictures from the delivery room a few minutes after it happened. Someone was celebrating the fourth birthday of their daughter with a Doraemon cake. Someone had posted pictures of a brand new suit ruined because their child ran a scissors through it. It was like the whole world was just producing babies. No wonder we have such a population problem, he thought.

To Anmol, there seemed to be only one really happy guy on his time line and he was still a bachelor, enjoying life travelling across the world, scuba diving in Singapore, pub-hopping in Sydney, going on Jamaican cruises with his American girlfriend. He wondered if he had rushed into getting married at the young age of twenty-six.

Anmol decided to head for office. He changed into the formal clothes, walked to his car in the massive hospital parking lot, got in his Fortuner and started the drive towards his office. It was already close to six in the morning. He would be gone a few hours and be back by noon. The hospital anyway had his phone number in case they needed to reach him.

The drive was thirty minutes long. He turned on the radio, hoping for some good music to kill the time. As luck would have it, it was Children's Day and the RJ was talking about children and parenthood. One woman was describing her experiences and how motherhood changed her life. She talked for five minutes about how she thought that her child was God's gift to her and how even a glance at her made her heart feel warm. Anmol turned the radio off.

'We will name him Parikshit if it's a boy, and Naina if we have a daughter,' Komal had announced, after spending about two months researching names. She had been euphoric all through the pregnancy, while Anmol had spent sleepless nights tossing and turning in the bed.

His mind just kept going over what was going to happen next. *One day she will start going to school. Maybe she will be disciplined and studious. Maybe she will be a tomboy like her mother. What if she gets into fights with boys? What if boys chase her all the time, taking rounds of our apartment building hoping for a glimpse of her?* He knew he had done this with Komal, albeit when they both were in college.

What if it's a boy? Girls are still easier to manage. Boys tend to be difficult. What if he's a womaniser? What if he doesn't want to study at all? I won't hesitate to smack him if he misbehaves.

What will they do when they grow up? Engineering? Medicine? Regardless of what people may say, these are still the best possible career options. If he has to do engineering, we need to get him into a good coaching class from class 10. No, these days they start from class 8. God, who knows, maybe they will start from class 6 by the time he gets there. Poor kid. No, it will be tough on us too. What if I have a presentation to make the next day and he needs help with physics or organic chemistry? The competition would be terrible by the time they sit for the IIT JEE. Ten, maybe twenty lakh students taking the exam. How will our child even have any chance? What will he do? Maybe we will just send him abroad. Harvard, probably. Yes, I need to start doubling my saving if we have to send him to Harvard. There is anyway no future in India.

What about marriage? What if he comes back saying that he wants to marry an American girl? Will she want to live with us desi people? Will Komal and I end up spending our last days in some old age home while our boy spends his time with his American wife? Oh my God, no no, he will take the IIT JEE. We will find a nice Indian girl for him on shaadi.com.

'*Bride wanted for handsome Punjabi boy. Caste, creed, no bar. Seeking well-educated girl from good family. We don't believe in dowry.*' He drafted the matrimonial ad in his mind.

His phone rang. It was his sister.

'Anmol, how is Komal? What happened?'

'Hello Di. Komal is in the delivery room. The doctor confirmed that she is in labour, but it might take some time.'

'*Achha*, okay. You must be in the waiting area? Are you okay? Feeling excited?'

Anmol blew his horn at a car coming towards him from the wrong side. It went by, missing him narrowly.

'Anmol, where are you? Are you driving?'

He sighed. 'Yes, just thought of going to the office for a quick break. Had some work to wrap up.'

She shouted so loudly that Anmol had to move the phone away, lest his eardrums rupture.

'ARE YOU CRAZY? YOUR WIFE IS IN THE HOSPITAL ALONE AND YOU ARE GOING TO THE OFFICE?'

'Relax Di. She is in good hands. Besides, I was getting bored there. I had nothing to do.'

'Anmol, this is just not done. You need to stop behaving like a stupid child and take care of your wife and child. Now go back and call me when you are at the hospital. I don't have anything else to say to you.' She slammed the phone down.

Anmol slowed down, but kept going. He used to call his sister a drama-queen and was quite used to her outbursts.

He was driving next to a park now. The sun was almost up and there were people walking about, out for their morning exercise. He noticed a father-son duo nearby. The boy was a little older than the one at the hospital, maybe six or seven years old. He was learning to ride a bicycle. Anmol decided to stop for a minute to watch.

The father was pushing the cycle as the boy rode it. As he gathered momentum, the father let go of the cycle.

The child kept going for a couple of seconds, but noticed that he no longer had the support and fell down, grazing his knee. His dad ran up to him, picked him up, hugged him, gave him a kiss on the cheek, and sat him down on the cycle again. This time, he didn't support him by his shoulders but held the rear of the cycle, so that he doesn't realise when he lets go.

They followed the same pattern, the dad let go eventually, but the boy continued cycling and kept going on, for a much longer duration this time. He fell again eventually when he came across a jogger coming in his direction, but he had been successful. Anmol had to crane his neck to follow the proceedings but noticed that this time there were no tears in his eyes, just sheer joy. His dad came running over to him and gave him a tight hug. His eyes shone with love and pride at this little achievement of his son. Just watching them gave Anmol a warm, fuzzy feeling. He hadn't felt that proud even when he got his last promotion. *Maybe this was the reason Yadav was always so happy talking about his children's achievements.*

Anmol turned the car key, switched on the right indicator, took a U-turn and headed back to the hospital. The CEO's presentation could wait.

৪০৫৪

A WHISPERED PRAYER

NIKITA SINGH

People change. Every person is a summation of every single thing he has done in his life, every single thing that has happened to him and every single thing he has experienced or observed happening around him. We choose to leave some things behind, and we move on, have new experiences, therefore changing with time. But it all counts. It makes us who we are.

'Welcome to Lotus Appliances! How may I help you?' Anjali asked politely. She got engrossed in her phone call, troubleshooting, and looked up only when her colleague tapped on her shoulder. Anjali placed her hand over the phone, covering the receiver and raised her eyebrow questioningly.

Pratibha mouthed, 'Did you hear?'

Instantly, Anjali knew what this was about. Everyone had been waiting for this day since a long time, and engrossed in her work, it had momentarily slipped Anjali's headspace. But now, her heart started beating loudly in her chest—so loud that she could barely hear what Pratibha said next. 'I'm sorry, what?' she asked.

'Death penalty to all four of those bastards,' Pratibha repeated. 'Well deserved. If anything, those beasts got away easy. They should be tortured before they're hung till death. Or better yet—handed over to the public; we'd take care of them in our way.'

Anjali was numb.

'Sadly, though, death penalty is the highest grade of punishment the Indian law permits. But at least they made a verdict, and that too within nine months. That's unheard of, right?'

Anjali had stopped listening. They won. The fight, which had become India's fight... She was overwhelmed with emotion. Everything she had kept coiled up inside her unreeled. She finally let herself believe that there still was hope. That people were changing, the society was changing, India was coming forward and protesting openly and fiercely against crimes against women. It was no longer a taboo to mention them in public. And most importantly, such protests and demonstrations have actually begun to have an impact on how these cases are handled. Government, the law—everybody was sitting up and paying attention to what's been going on and the injustice of it all.

16 December, 2012 created a revolution in the country. As the news of what's been popularly termed as 'Delhi

Gang Rape' spread around the nation like wildfire, it brought thousands and thousands of people out on the streets, demanding justice. Justice for the girl who had been held against her will, beaten brutally and gang raped by six men on a moving bus, right in the middle of the capital city of India.

When the incident hit the news the next day, it created a rampage around the country. Lakhs of people signed online petitions, thousands participated in protest marches and demonstrations in every state of the country. The horrible incident shook India.

People term rape-victims who manage to stay alive 'survivors'. In that sense, Anjali was a survivor too, even though she never felt like one. She constantly kept looking around to check if somebody was following her, always took the busiest of streets, never stepped out alone at night and double checked all the doors and windows every night before sleep. She'd been disintegrating slowly, falling apart into pieces, one bit at a time, since a long time...but Nirbhaya gave her hope.

Maybe India was, in fact, waking up.

৪০৫৪

On her way back home, Anjali looked out of the cab's window at the fascinating city that is Kolkata. Half of the city is historic, the other half ultra-modern—there is no in-between. You can go seamlessly from centuries old monuments built during the period when the British ruled over India, to top-notch modern day architecture in the blink of an eye. She especially enjoyed these evening rides in her company's official cab (in safe custody of four of her colleagues) looking out at the city after an honest day's work. Every morning, her husband accompanied her on her way to the office, at the office she was surrounded by hundreds of people and in the cab back home, she was surrounded by people too, but the place she felt safest at was her home. Ever since her rape, over two years ago, she has been in a constant state of alertness. Something about going back home, after having gone through another day without breaking down, calmed her perpetually jittery nerves.

She took the elevator to her floor and let herself into the apartment. She quickly scanned her home for invaders, keeping her cell phone ready in her hand, prepared to raise an alarm if anything seemed amiss. Another part of her routine. Satisfied, she dropped her handbag on the bed and went to freshen up in the washroom. She was in an exceptionally good mood that day, ever since she got the news.

Twenty minutes later, when the doorbell rang, Anjali rushed to open it. She peeked through the magic eye and saw her husband waiting outside. She undid the latch and pulled the door open.

'I forgot my keys,' Sameer said.

'I know; I saw it on your desk. What's *that*?' she pointed to the large brown paper bag in her husband's hand.

'Just something from work. I told you about this new prototype, didn't I? I've to test it once over the weekend and—'

'Never mind. I won't understand a word of what you say anyway, so—'

'What smells good?' Sameer asked and walked towards the kitchen, following the aroma of tandoori chicken.

'We had some chicken in the freezer, I thought I'd surprise you since I got home early, but you ruined it by coming early too!'

'A wife that resents me coming home from work early. Now I *truly* have everything.'

'Shut up!' Anjali punched Sameer's arm playfully and crinkled her nose. As she went to the stove to check on the chicken, he followed her there and wrapped his arm around her from behind, resting his chin on her shoulder. When he felt her face grow hot, he nibbled softly on her ear. 'Stop, you're making me burn the chicken,' Anjali whispered.

'I don't care. Multitask.'

'You're mean.'

Sameer turned her towards him and kissed her softly on the lips. 'Is *that* mean?'

'*Stopping* that is mean,' she pulled him back towards her.

Anjali drew an unhealthy amount of strength and support from Sameer. They were co-dependant, like every other couple madly in love with each other is, but for Anjali,

Sameer was a life source. She couldn't, for one second, even try to imagine existing in a world without him. She simply couldn't. He was there with her during her darkest times, he had stayed up nights with her, he'd held her through her nightmares, he'd fought the world for her and every time she stumbled, he'd been there with her to keep her from falling. He was the reason she woke up every morning. He was the reason she fought. Being around him, she forgot everything that was wrong with her life. Being with him, she felt normal.

ॐ

'Get up,' Sameer whispered in her ears.

She moaned and adjusted herself against him more comfortably.

'Anjali, wake *up*!'

'No,' she groaned. But she opened one eye to see what was going on. There was light, which hurt her eye, so she shut it again. Then what she'd seen registered and she opened both her eyes and sat up on the bed. 'What...?'

There was a heart shaped velvet cake and a bunch of pink roses laid out on a breakfast table on Sameer's side of the bed. Two small candles were fixed into the cake and lit. And Sameer was wearing a wide goofy grin on his face. 'Happy anniversary,' he said, in a sing-song voice. '*Two years*, baby!'

She giggled.

'Say it back!' he insisted.

'But we...we don't celebrate anniversaries...' she studied his face, half lit and beautiful from the glow of candlelight. She had always been a fan of his strong square jaw line and gentle eyes.

'We do now. We've decided to move on and leave the past behind. So, happy anniversary!' Sameer beamed at her.

'Happy anniversary! This is *so* sweet!' Anjali launched herself at him and hugged him tight.

'Whoa, careful. Candles around, we don't want to burn our house down!'

'Way to make a romantic moment even more romantic,' she said and let go of him. She picked up the bouquet of flowers and keeping it close to her nose, she inhaled.

'There's artificial perfume in that thing. Also, can we please cut the cake now? I'm hungry!'

'Seriously. You *couldn't* be more romantic,' Anjali shook her head and picked up the plastic knife that came with the cake. She cut a slice and fed it to Sameer.

'Mmm, yummy! Try it,' as he fed some of it to her, he saw her looking at him intently. He knew that look. She was thinking about everything they had been through. She was slipping to her dark place again.

'Happy anniversary,' she murmured, with tears in her eyes. 'You mean so much...without you...'

'Shh,' he put a finger on her lips to shut her up. 'I know, I know,' he nodded and hugged her. He held her close to himself for a minute and rocked her against his chest. Then, he said, 'You know...when I said I was hungry, I wasn't lying. This cake really does—'

With that, Anjali burst out laughing, and cut him a big slice, a wide smile plastered on her face. They stayed up and chatted for a long time. Lying in his arms, she felt secure. The only way she could sleep at nights, was knowing that he was right beside her and no matter what happens, he would always be right beside her.

శోఆ

'We should go home,' Anjali suggested. She had been thinking about it for a long time, and finally gathered enough courage to say it out loud.

Sameer, who had just come out of the shower, was stunned. He froze on spot and asked, '*What?*'

'It's been two years, Sameer. We should go home and meet our parents.'

'We're not talking about this. It's not even up for discussion.'

'But...at least listen to me. They were scared. They didn't know what to do,' Anjali tried to explain.

'So were you. They couldn't have been more scared than you. No one can be as scared as you were. I was there. I saw it. I'm not going to let you put yourself through that again,' Sameer said, his jaw tight.

'It's been years. I've been thinking about this, and I think... things change. People change.'

'No, they don't. At least people like your parents and mine... they don't change. They stick to their traditional distorted beliefs and will never even try to understand...' Sameer shook his head. 'You know them; they are...'

'Yes, but they are our *parents*. Everything happened so suddenly; it must've been such a shock for them. Maybe now that they've had time to think, they'll...accept us.'

Sameer snorted.

'Please, Sameer. We cut all ties and ran away. We can't leave things like that. Even if they do not accept us, we should at least ask for forgiveness.'

'*Forgiveness?* What did *we* do wrong...?'

Anjali tried to convince Sameer that it was time they let the past go and go back to their parents. She gave all kinds of reasons, made excuses for their behaviour, she begged and pleaded, but Sameer was extremely opposed to the idea of trying to make things right with their parents. In the end, Anjali told him that if he didn't come with her, she would go alone.

'You can't go alone! And nothing good can come out of this...'

'Sameer, things have changed. People talk about these things openly now. Maybe they regret everything and want to get in touch with us, but we've left no trace?'

Anjali stepped in front of him and made him look at her. 'We should at least try. Just once. I promise I won't mention it ever again if this doesn't go well.'

He looked at her and stayed silent for a minute. 'I don't understand why you'd want to put yourself through all that shit again...' he muttered, but Anjali knew he would give in.

'I just...I want some closure. I really feel I can move on from everything. And for that, I need to face them and just...mend things with them...' she struggled to make him understand.

He took a long breath and sighed. 'Okay.'

'Okay?'

'Okay. If this means so much to you.'

ॐ

Not much had changed in Ara in the past two years. In fact, everything in the village felt exactly the same to them. They took an auto rickshaw to her parents' place, without haggling with the driver for overcharging; they had more important concerns. They stayed silent for the twenty minutes it took the auto to reach the front gate of the house Anjali had spent most of her life in. When it stopped, neither of them stepped out.

The auto driver turned to them, 'We've reached.'

Sameer nodded, and took out his wallet to pay him. Anjali peeked out; her mother was out in the front yard, laying down laundry on the grass to dry. She took a deep breath and stepped out of the auto.

'I've got a bad feeling about this,' Sameer muttered to himself. '*Bhaiya*, could you wait here for five minutes?'

'Where do you want to go next?' the driver asked.

'I don't know yet. Just wait for five minutes, I'll let you know.'

'Okay.'

He heard her before he saw her. As Sameer stepped out of the auto, he heard Anjali's mother say, '*You...?* What are you doing here?'

'Maa...' Anjali said, walking towards her mother, tears in her eyes. What Sameer wouldn't give to spare Anjali this pain and just take her back home. Instead, he took a deep breath and went to stand by her side.

'Anjali, go away! What were you *thinking* coming back here?' her mother whispered furiously, loud enough for Anjali to hear, but not the neighbours. Family's honour being more important than her own flesh and blood and everything.

'I came to see you all. How are you? How is everybody...?'

'It's none of your business!' her mother hissed.

'It's my *family*!' Anjali pleaded with her mother to understand. 'I miss you. I miss everybody. And I'm so sorry...but it's been so long...can't you just forgive me?'

'*Forgive* you? You disgraced us. You ruined our family name. And if that wasn't enough, you have come back to—'

'What's going on here?' Anjali's father came out of the house, hearing the commotion. As soon as he saw Anjali and Sameer, his face hardened. 'YOU!' he thundered.

Anjali looked around helplessly. A crowd was beginning to gather. People on the road were slowing down, neighbours were peeking in. 'I think it's best if we go inside to...' Sameer began, but was cut off by Anjali's father.

'DON'T YOU DARE TAKE A STEP INTO MY HOUSE!' he thundered. 'GET OUT. GET OFF MY PROPERTY!'

Sameer looked at Anjali, but when she didn't budge, he stayed by her too.

'Papa, we're sorry. We're so sorry for everything we put you through. We just want everything to be okay again. I know we made a mistake, but I'm still your daughter, papa please...' Anjali begged.

'YOU'RE *NOT* MY DAUGHTER. YOU'VE ONLY BROUGHT SHAME TO US.'

'But papa, we had no choice... You weren't letting us get married, and you weren't happy with me staying with you here either...'

'So you should have killed yourself,' her mother interjected.

'Maa!' Anjali's younger brother had come out too, and was looking torn between what he was supposed to do—be a silent observer, and what he wanted to do—run to the elder sister he hadn't seen in two years.

'Shut up and go inside!' both his parents turned to him and screamed at the same time.

'Papa...' Anjali sobbed.

'Let's just go,' Sameer held her elbow and tried to guide her back, but she still didn't budge.

'I'm *not* your father. You mother is right. First you go out and shame the family's honour, and then...you have the guts to tell us you want to marry this son of a bitch?'

'He's a good person and I love him. He's been with me through all of this when you weren't there...'

'Because you are nothing to us now! You're dead to us!' her mother yelled. Now, that the volume of the exchange had increased, the mob was even more interested in the drama.

'But I didn't do anything...it wasn't my fault...'

'Why did you need to step out of the house? Nothing would've happened if you had stayed home,' her father said.

'We should never have sent you to Patna to study. You forgot your own limits,' her mother added.

'*How can you even*...?' Anjali looked from her mother to her father and back again. As her brain tried to understand what her parents had just accused her of, she started breathing hard, fighting the urge to hit someone or throw something. For the first time since she got there, she was furious. 'Are you...? Are you seriously blaming *me* for what happened to me? It wasn't *my* fault. How could you even think that? How can you...?'

She kept shaking her head, trying to understand her parents' twisted, prejudiced thought process.

'Of course we blame you! Who else will we blame? You were the one who—' her father started, but Sameer shut him up.

'Stop it. Just stop it, both of you. You make me *sick*,' Sameer ground his teeth in anger, holding Anjali's hand. She was shaking with fury. She had been crying before, when she was trying to explain to her parents why she eloped with Sameer, but when they started blaming her for her own rape, that's when she lost her temper. Her tears dried in her eyes, as she was overcome with revulsion.

'Let's go, Sameer. You were right—this is not worth it,' she said, glaring at her bigoted parents.

'No, these people disgust me. They are blaming you for getting raped. They are the ones who should've been by your side, and helped you through it. But instead, they made you keep it a secret, fearing what? The society?' he threw his hands around and pointed at the people gathered there. 'Do you think these people *respect* you for asking your own daughter to commit suicide? Instead of filing a police report and trying to find the bastard who did this to her, you just wanted to get rid of her, didn't you? That night she came back...' Sameer shook his head.

'*Get off my property*,' Anjali's father sneered.

'You think I *want* to be here? We were happy. I was helping Anjali, and she was getting better. We have a normal life, we have a *good* life. But she wanted to come here and meet you, because even though you want her dead, she's your daughter and she's biologically programmed to love you. But you people...you don't love anything except your honour. When your daughter came home in that state, you wanted her to die. You wanted her off your hands, so that no one ever got to know that a woman from your *prestigious* family was raped. Instead of demanding justice for her, instead of being her parents and taking care of her... And anyway, it's one thing to not report a case to the police and keep it hidden in fear of social rejection or whatever. But you actually *blamed* her, you *despised* her for getting raped, as if she'd made a voluntary decision. I think you were secretly glad that she told you about me right after that incident—you found a reason to hate her. And when we ran away, we made your job easier...' Sameer spat on the ground. 'It's good that we came. Now she knows what kind of people you are. She has been dead to you since a long time, and now, after this—you can finally be dead to her.'

With that, he turned around and pulled Anjali with him. The auto rickshaw was still there, waiting for them. Who would miss such a show? Sameer got in after Anjali and held her to him, instructing the auto driver to take them back to the railway station.

They waited at the station for hours, until a train that followed their route finally arrived. On their journey back, Anjali didn't say anything. She didn't cry. She didn't even look at anything. She just sat still, staring blankly at her hands, which she kept in her lap, entwined with Sameer's hand.

৯০৩

When they got home a little past midnight, Sameer went straight to take a shower, while Anjali changed and fixed something to eat. She boiled instant noodles, and sat down next to the stove on the cold granite counter with a sigh. She didn't understand how she felt about everything that happened; it was a lot to process and her feelings were jumbled. When Sameer came out of the shower, the noodles was done. He poured it all into a large bowl and grabbed a couple of forks. Anjali followed him to their bedroom.

They sat down on the floor, resting their backs against the bed and dug into their dinner. They were both silent, deep into their lines of thoughts.

'So...*that* didn't go very well,' Sameer sighed suddenly and dramatically.

Anjali giggled and looked at him. The light moment lasted only a few seconds, before they got silent again; they both knew they were thinking about the same thing and that they were going to have to talk about it. 'I just...I had been concentrating so much on meeting them and asking for forgiveness for eloping and getting married, I never thought they blamed me for getting raped. They hate us.'

'I hate them.'

'Don't say that.'

'It's true,' Sameer emphasised.

'We...let's not talk about this. I *can't*. Not yet.' Anjali's expression looked pained. Sameer nodded silently and they finished dinner.

෨෬

The next morning, Sameer left for office early to attend a meeting, but Anjali slept in. She got up when her maid, Vimla, rang the doorbell. While the maid did the dishes and mopped the floor, Anjali took a shower and got dressed. She put on grey trousers, with an off white shirt and was in the process of deciding which shoes to wear, when Vimla came in to mop the bedroom.

'I came here yesterday, nobody opened the door. Had you gone somewhere?' Vimla asked.

'Yes, we went...home.' It felt odd to refer to that place as *home* now.

'Oh. Is it okay if I don't come tomorrow? I have to take my son to get him some shots.'

'Yes, of course. How old is he?' Anjali inquired.

'Almost a year now. He's started walking; I feel so proud!'

They made small talk for a while. Even though they were talking about Vimla, Anjali's mind was in a whole another world. She phased out, nodding her head, but not actually hearing anything Vimla was saying. When Anjali shut the door after Vimla had left, she sort of just...broke.

The impact of everything that happened hit her straight in the face. She got out of her work clothes and put on the loose T-shirt Sameer wore to sleep the previous night. She shut all the windows, turned all the lights off and went to the darkest corner of her bedroom and slumped on the floor, hugging her knees to her chest.

The way Vimla spoke about her son...that's how parents are supposed to feel about their children. Anjali wondered if Vimla had been as proud if her child was a girl. Maybe, maybe not. But she sure as hell would not hate her daughter the way Anjali's parents hated her. No overprotective parent in India can be blamed for being overprotective, given the circumstances. But if something bad does happen to their daughters, they help them through it, don't they? They don't blame it on their daughters and throw them out of their lives.

A sob escaped her lips, as she thought about the hurtful things her parents had said to her. *You should've killed yourself. You're dead to us!* Maybe...she should have. And she certainly would have, if not for Sameer. Anjali was taken back to that night...when it all began, and her association with her family ended.

When Anjali's parents had started thinking about getting her married, Sameer and Anjali had decided to tell their parents about their wish to marry each other. They knew that given their caste disparity, it was going to be tough to convince their parents, but they were foolish—they were in love.

But fate had other plans for them. The evening that they had planned to talk to their respective parents, Anjali had gone to one of her high school friends' place to congratulate her on her new born baby boy. At that time, Anjali had considered herself lucky to have parents who encouraged her to go for higher education after passing out of school and didn't force her to get married and start having babies. Meanwhile, Sameer had told his parents about Anjali and the heated Hindu-Muslim debate that ensued led to Sameer packing his bags and leaving home. He went to a friend's place and waited for Anjali's call to find out her parents' reaction.

When Anjali left her friend's house, she had decided to walk to the nearest auto stand, which was only a two minutes' walk. It was getting dark and there was no electricity since the last couple of hours. She was just about twenty steps away from the auto stand, when someone held her waist from behind and used his other hand to gag her and stop her from screaming. She kicked and struggled, but couldn't get out of the man's tight hold. He dragged her forcefully and once they were away from the road and into a secluded spot, he punched her several times. Anjali protested; she screamed, she bit and hit him and was even successful in kneeing him once, but that only angered him and made him kick her down on the dirty ground and beat her till she was barely conscious.

She could still hear the sound of her clothes ripping. She remembered how she begged and pleaded that man to let her go, and how he pinned both her hands above her head using one hand and laughed every time she winced in pain. When she passed out, he spit on her face to wake her up. He was not just doing it to fulfil whatever masochistic sexual desire he couldn't control; he was also a sadist. Seeing her in pain, seeing her alternate between fighting back and begging gave him pleasure. At that moment, she prayed to God to kill her. She couldn't take it anymore; she wanted it to end. And she knew that even after this beast had had his way with her, for her, it would not end. For her, it would never end.

After he was done, her put on his clothes and wiped off his sweat and left. He didn't even look down at her to see what he had done. Maybe his fill of sadism for the day had been satisfied. Anjali lay there in her blood and urine. She could hear her phone ringing consistently, but she didn't have the energy to get up and look for it. She passed out.

When her consciousness returned, her phone was still ringing. She got up slowly, looking for her clothes. She put on whatever was left of it and found her cell phone ringing in one of the dried weeds nearby. It was Sameer. She began crying, just seeing his name on her cell phone screen. Huge sobs wrecked her body, and her knees gave out. She fell to the floor, holding her phone in her hand, gathering courage to take the call, wondering what she would tell him...how she would explain to him what she had been put through...

When she finally pressed the answer button, Sameer's

panicked voice questioned hurriedly, 'Anjali? Where are you? Do you know how worried I have been? I thought something went wrong at your place. I thought you told your family, and you fought. So I came here, but you're not here... Where are you?'

Anjali sobbed into the phone, hearing concern and panic in Sameer's voice. She struggled to explain what happened, but no words came out. She somehow explained to him where she was and what had happened, her body convulsing as she cried.

When Sameer saw her, he took off his shirt to cover her up. He sat down with her and held her tight, first asking what happened, but when he realised it only tortured her more, he just hugged her silently. He called a friend and asked him to bring a car. They drove Anjali home. While the other two boys left immediately after reaching her place, Sameer picked her up and carried her inside.

Anjali's mother came out rushing. When Sameer had come to ask about Anjali's whereabouts a couple hours ago, she'd gotten worried too. She'd sent her son to pick Anjali up from her friend's place. But he had come back, saying she'd left there over an hour ago. Since then, her family had been searching for her frantically. When she saw her daughter, it took her seconds to decipher what must've happened. Instead of going to Anjali and seeing if she was okay, she ran to her bedroom, crying out for her husband.

Anjali spent the next few days lying in her bed, crying, crying and crying. No one spoke to her. She could hear her mother weeping in the other room, and assumed she was crying about her daughter's pain. Instead, she had only been concerned about how they would show their faces in public. Almost a week later, her mother finally spoke to her. She came to her room late one evening, and sat down at the foot of Anjali's bed. And she said, 'Why does that Muslim boy keep coming here? The neighbours have started asking questions.'

When Anjali told her mother that she loved Sameer and wanted to marry him, her mother immediately fetched her husband. After a whole lot of yelling and cursing, blaming their stars for ever giving birth to her, her parents took away her cell phone and locked her up in her room. They did not let Sameer visit after that.

After three days of being locked up in her room, Anjali heard a tap on her window at night. At first she was scared. She imagined her rapist coming for her again. But then she heard Sameer call out her name. They ran away that night, taking the first train out and changing trains three times on the way, they finally reached Kolkata. They stayed in a motel for a few days, after which they rented a one bedroom apartment. One week later, they went to a court and got married.

They were running out of money, and even though Sameer did not want to leave Anjali alone, he joined his office. All day, while he worked, Anjali locked herself in and did not so much as peek out of the window. When he came back from work every evening, she would hold onto him for dear life. The first few months were especially hard. The first time she stepped out of home was three months after they had rented it. Sameer's job was paying him well, and they started buying furniture and setting up a home.

Through their first year in Kolkata, all Anjali did every day was cook and clean. And when she wasn't doing that, she read about rape and rape cases on the internet. She was obsessed. Statistics say that one rape case happens in India, every twenty minutes. Around twenty five thousand cases are registered in the country every year, though unreported cases are believed to be much much higher than reported. She read about social rejection, about cases where parents married off their nineteen year old 'tainted' daughter to a fifty five year old divorcee with three children. She tried to justify her parents' decision to keep what happened to her a secret.

Not reporting a case is better than reporting it only to get insulted by police officials, who refuse to file reports, sometimes asking for proof of rape by undressing in front of them, raising fingers on the character of the victim, for being out alone at night, or dressing provocatively, or secretly enjoying the rape. If they do file a report, the chances of finding the rapist and the case ever reaching a court is very minimal, especially if the victim does not have political or monetary reach and the rapist has influence. Anjali read a case about a family breaking ties with the victim because instead of settling for the money offered by her rapist, she wanted to press charges.

She read about these cases, and she felt blessed. She felt that she had tormented her parents enough, and thought it was a good decision to not file a police case and not putting herself and her family through what would've followed. At that point of time, she honestly thought her parents were scared and confused and on top of that, when they got to know about Sameer, they flipped out. She had always thought that one day, she would go back home, and they would take her back.

And when Nirbhaya's case came up, she saw hope. Nirbhaya and her family had helped discouraging the social stigma to a great extent. Anjali took strength from them.

All the hope that news had given Anjali now lay shattered on the floor, where she sobbed uncontrollably. People change, and she had hoped that since India has started opening up about crime against women, her parents would also understand what had been done to their daughter. And she had hoped they would forgive them for eloping. It had taken her two years to recover enough to go back to that village...and she had been concentrating so much about her parents, she had forgotten about her rape. It was when she was there, and the train stopped, that she realised where she was, and what had happened to her in that village.

Even after that, she had been strong and continued. She had met her parents, and they had rejected her again—only this time, she knew she had been rejected, and unlike last time, she did not have a hope of reconciliation she could hang on to.

She had put the broken pieces of her life together. She had gotten over most of her fear and paranoia, she had stepped out and gotten a job. She had built a family of her own—a stable, loving relationship with her husband. She had friends and colleagues and hobbies. She had even planned to switch jobs and do something that really interested her. She prayed every night, whispering a prayer to God, to help her fight. Every day was a battle. And then, pursuing the false hope Nirbhaya had given her, she had gone back home. And now, she found herself back to square one.

'Anjali...'

She looked up to see Sameer standing at the door in darkness. 'Sameer.'

He came to her and sat beside her. 'You weren't taking my calls. You know you can't do that.'

'I do. I'm sorry...' He nodded. As he sat there on the floor with her, she poured her heart out, she told him everything she had been feeling, how depressed she was, and how she desperately she had wanted everything to work out with their parents. 'You didn't even go to see your parents...'

'After what happened with yours...I knew how it would go with mine. It's useless,' Sameer said.

'But, I thought...people change, so maybe...'

'No, Anjali. People change, yes, but only if they want to. Only if they try to open their minds.'

'I tried so hard to forget what happened...but in Ara, it all came back. I pretend it never happened, that I was never raped, and I am okay for some time, but then, one day out of the blue, it all comes back to me and I break down...' Anjali said.

'That's the thing, Anjali—you *can't* forget what happened. You can't. You want to, and I want you to, but it is not possible. It wasn't something inconsequential. We don't like it, but it is a part of your life, it is a part of who you are. It's a big enough part to define whatever you do and how you do it. But we can't let it grow bigger. And I think...I think the only way to move on from that is to accept that it happened. Then we'll get to a point where it will no longer define who we are.'

'But, how?' Anjali looked up to him, with tears in her eyes. But also hope. It made him hopeful too.

'I don't know how. But maybe, with time... We feel shitty right now, but don't you think we feel less shitty than we did two years ago? Soon, we'll have more experiences— hopefully good, and certainly not as bad. As the bits and pieces add up, our new experiences will overtake the old, shitty ones, and one day...we'll be okay.'

They stayed silent for some time. The more she thought about what Sameer said, the more Anjali was convinced she could do it. With him by her side, she could definitely do it.

'We'll be okay?'

Sameer pulled her towards him and rested his head on her shoulder. 'What do you think?'

She ran her fingers through his hair. 'We'll be okay.'

And then, they sat there for a long time, Sameer coming up with all sorts of scenarios from their future together—their kids, their first car, their own house and the places they wanted to visit. They chose what they would wear, and where she would shop from. And as they painted a beautiful picture of their future, Anjali swore to herself that she would not give up till she left her past behind. With Sameer by her side, she knew she could.

ॐ

Meenakshi Reddy Madhavan is the author of *You Are Here* and *Cold Feet*, both bestselling novels. She also wrote the young adult novel *The Life & Times of Layla The Ordinary* under the name Minna Madhavan for younger readers.

Meenakshi has been writing from the time she was a young girl, and began her now famous blog *Compulsive Confessions* at twenty-two. The blog is ten years old, and gets approximately 40,000 hits per month—a massive first for a personal blog in India.

Meenakshi was featured as one of the women of the year in a leading national daily and she was also one of Airtel's featured youth in a campaign they did for ThinkFest.

She also works as a lifestyle journalist and freelancer and has been with three major publications in the past. At the moment, Meenakshi is working on her next book, juggling multiple deadlines, and working to feed her fat ginger cat: TC. She lives in New Delhi and Mumbai with her partner.

Durjoy Datta was born in New Delhi and completed a degree in engineering and business management before embarking on a writing career. His first book—*Of Course I Love You!*—was published when he was twenty-one years old and was an instant bestseller. His successive novels—*Now That You're Rich!, She Broke Up, I Didn't!, Ohh Yes, I Am Single!, If It's Not Forever, Till the Last Breath, Someone Like You* and *Hold My Hand*—have made him one of the highest selling authors in India.

In 2009, he was recognised as a young achiever by *The Times of India*. He was chosen as one of the two young achievers in the field of media and communications by Whistling Woods International in 2011 and was one of the recipients of the Teacher's Achievement Awards in 2012.

Durjoy is currently based at Mumbai, where he writes a hugely popular sitcom *Saada Haq* for Channel V. He loves dogs and is an active Crossfitter. You can follow him on Twitter (*@durjoydatta*) or Facebook (*www.facebook.com/durjoydatta1*).

Judy Balan writes romantic-comedy. More comedy than romance, she insists. It's more like a deconstruction of the romantic-comedy, really. So while her stories are sometimes part romantic, she gets her kick out of taking digs at romance as a genre. This is why both her novels have a distinct anti-romance thing going for them and not because she's turned into 'Bitter Divorced Lady' who likes to burst everyone's happily-ever-after bubbles.

She's also a compulsive theorist. You may hop over to her blog *www.womanandaquarter.blogspot.com* to find all her theories, ranging from the profound to the delightfully superficial.

Judy is the author of the bestselling *Two Fates: The Story of My Divorce* and *Sophie Says: Memoirs of a Breakup Coach*. She's currently working on her third novel (a comedy about death) and her first sitcom. She also writes plays, columns, blogs and enjoys testing her skills across mediums and talking about herself in the third person. Judy and her daughter Kiara, live in Chennai.

Harsh Snehanshu is twenty-four but looks older. He studied at IIT where he barely passed and went on to start-up a venture at which he most definitely failed. He then devoted a year and a half to travel across the country on a shoestring budget, sleeping wherever there was space and eating whatever was available. He has a wealth of stories to tell which can be accounted for by the wealth of grey hair he has. He loves to paint, sing and play any musical instrument that he chances upon. He enjoys telling stories, real or mostly otherwise, to those interested at TEDx and college festivals.

The author of *Because Shit Happened: What Not To Do In A Start-up!* and the bestselling *Kanav-Tanya trilogy*, Harsh currently is back to school as a Young India Fellow. You can read his columns in *The Hindu* and *Tehelka*.

Shoma Narayanan started reading romances at the age of eleven, borrowing them from neighbours, and hiding them inside textbooks so that her parents didn't find out. At that time, the thought of writing one herself never entered her head—she was convinced she wanted to be a teacher when she grew up. Like most childhood dreams, that one didn't come true (sigh), and she ended up becoming a banker instead.

Three years ago, Shoma took up writing as a hobby (after successively trying her hand at baking, sewing, knitting, crochet and patchwork), and was amazed at how much she enjoyed it. To her own surprise, she ended up being Mills & Boon's first Indian author to be published internationally. She's had four novels published so far, and has three more releasing in 2014. Her family has been unfailingly supportive of her latest hobby, and are also secretly very, very relieved that they don't have to eat, wear or display the results!

Parinda Joshi is a technology enthusiast by day, a writer by night, and a caffeine-based life form in between. Born and raised in Ahmedabad, she's often found making small talk on a flight between the entertainment capital of the world, Los Angeles, and the geek hub, Silicon Valley, trying to juggle her interests and family.

Parinda is the author of two novels that couldn't be more different from each other; *Live from London* and *Powerplay*. She has contributed to publications like *The South Asian Times* and *GQ* on a variety of topics—music, technology and trends that affect South Asians globally.

She indulges in reading, photography, people-watching and biking with her husband when she's not busy being outwitted by her five-year-old daughter.

She tweets at *@randomwalkers* and there isn't a Gujju joke in Twitterverse that she hasn't heard. More about Parinda at her website (*www.parindajoshi.com*).

Atulya Mahajan is the proud father of two—an adorable young boy who has him mostly wrapped around his little finger, and a funny book called *Amreekandesi: Masters of America*, which came to life in 2013.

Atulya has been writing a popular satire blog at *amreekandesi.com* for many years now, and his greatest fear is someone important actually reading his blog-posts and shutting down the blog. His second greatest fear is driving. He has spent thousands of hours shouting at random taxi drivers and motorcyclists who overtake from the wrong side, more so when he is trying to tweet something profound while also keeping an eye on the road. Atulya's Twitter addiction has got him into a lot of trouble over the last few years, mostly from his mother and wife, who threaten to forfeit his phone any day now.

Atulya would write more often if only he didn't have to deal with the millions of fans who stalk him wherever he goes, in his dreams.

Nikita Singh was born in Patna and brought up in Indore, and was pursuing a bachelor's degree in pharmacy when she turned to writing. Her first book—*Love @ Facebook*—came out in May 2011, when she was nineteen years old, and since then, she has written many more novels—*Accidentally In Love, If It's Not Forever, The Promise, Someone Like You, Right Here Right Now*. She loves collaboration, and has written two novels with Durjoy Datta, a non-fiction title with Myshkin Ingawale (*The Unreasonable Fellows*) and edited an anthology of short stories (*25 Strokes of Kindness*) with Orvana Ghai. She has also contributed to the books of *The Backbenchers* series, *The Extra Class* and *The Missed Call*, co-authoring them with Durjoy, under a pen name.

With a library stocked with over 12,000 books, she is a voracious reader. A cricket enthusiast and a fitness freak, Nikita is based at New Delhi, where she works at a leading publishing house. Touch base with her on Twitter or Instagram (*@singh_nikita*) or Facebook (*www.facebook.com/nikitasingh.page*).